Kaytlin turned and stepped onto the emerald green of the plain. Two more careful steps and the wind slammed into her like a fist. It lasted only seconds, and then all was still. She took eight more steps, and the wind slammed into her, again. Jason walked to her left, a couple of steps behind. On the next lull, he came abreast of her, matching his pace to hers.

"I know what you are doing with Kraig. Don't use him to play me a fool." he snapped. She stopped, staring at him in astonishment.

"I don't need him to play you a fool, Jason. You do that well enough on your own!" she snarled, then spun on her heel and stalked away. She had gone several steps when she realized that she had forgotten to count.

Kathryn H. Sargeant   Blood Secrets: The Possession

This is a work of fiction. Any similarities between these characters and any persons living or dead are purely coincidental.

For my parents, Steve and Brenda. Thanks for teaching me to read. And to dream.

Copyright 2007

ISBN   978-0-615-17745-8

Kathryn H. Sargeant   Blood Secrets: The Possession

Blood Secrets: The Possession

By: Kathryn H. Sargeant

The flames leaped higher and higher, licking at the caves ceiling as the girl went on setting the room in order. She knew the kings were coming and she knew why. The foreseeing would take a lot of Amee, and herself as well, but was that not the price of being a priestess of Shondea, the great star seer? Her mind drifted back to the last time that her uncle, the king of Zemire, had come. Gregory had demanded that she return to their kingdom with him, but she had fled into the mountain and hid deep in its labyrinthine heart until he gave up and left without her.

She shook her head to clear aside the memories and brought her attention back to the matters at hand. "Please, Natahlia," she sighed, "my mother, help Amee to keep some of her strength. Please, keep my mentor and friend safe for I could not bear it to lose her, too. And give me strength to stand against Uncle Gregory. I know he will try to take me back to his kingdom, again." As she tossed more wood onto the fire, a gentle wind brushed through the room, bearing a sweet soft voice to her ears. A whisper only heard on the winds that blew through Caladren Mountain.

"The strength that you need you have always had. In times of trouble, look to the wolf." Her mothers' voice tickled at her earlobe. Kaytlin dropped the wood she had been carrying in a sudden wave of frustration

"If I have the strength," she demanded furiously of the air, "then why do I feel like a leaf at the mercy of a tempest? Why does my memory confuse me so? It mingles with my thoughts and creates a vortex that only allows uncertainty

7

and confusion to escape. I try to deny my feelings and do what comes instinctively, but daily life has become difficult because of the growing sense of dread that I feel. The star on my shoulder burns. I'm so confused. I just don't understand!"

"You will in time, my darling. Just allow the old knowledge that is your heritage to rise from inside and guide you." The wind caressed Kaytlin's tear stained cheek. "But, I sense you holding back. What is it?"

"I don't know. I feel something growing just beyond reach. It is weak, but there. And there have been more and more attacks on the people and disappearances. No one is safe. And the regents seem to think nothing of it. Almost as if the well being of their subjects were not their concern."

"The time is drawing near for the Circle to form, again. And this time it will not fall. Have patience, darling, and it will all reveal itself in time."

"I fear time is one thing we have both too much of and yet not near enough." Kaytlin swiped her hair from her eyes and quickly piled the scented wood next to the fire pit.

"Kaytlin?" Amee, the seeress, called from down the twisting corridors. "Go out and greet our guests, lest they try to enter alone and become hopelessly lost."

Always, the petitioner waited outside in the sacred clearing or by the lagoon while the question was asked and the answer sought. Kaytlin would deliver the message after it had been deciphered. But, not this time; this time the

Blood Secrets: The Possession

petitioners would be allowed into the holy seeing room, temple to Shondea herself.

"Yes, Amee. I am on my way," she called, glancing once more around the room and nodding curtly to herself in satisfaction. She turned and raced down the black corridors, fleet and sure-footed as a cat on the time worn stone. She stopped just short of the caves mouth to compose herself and then stepped out into the brilliant sunlight of a late autumn mid-day. Her midnight blue eyes adjusted instantly to the light and she bowed low to the two men standing in the clearing's center. Her shoulder length chestnut hair brushed the ground before she straightened to her full five foot seven inch height and smiled at them both. At the tender age of ten she was stunning and showed promise of becoming even more so. When she spoke, her soft and melodic voice seemed to be absorbed by the trees it touched.

"Your majesties, you honor us greatly. Please, allow me to guide you to the oracle." She lifted one of the heavy torches that were always burning from the bracket by the entrance and turned to lead the way. Silently, they traveled but Kaytlin felt his eyes on her spine, making her grow rigid. A ball of dread knotted in the pit of her stomach. Finally, when she thought she could bear the tension no longer, the silken curtain embroidered with the symbol of Shondea floated into view. Kaytlin swept it aside with relief and motioned them inside. Carefully, she set the torch in a niche then followed them.

Amee sat amongst the brightly colored pillows near the sacred flames. A timeless, ageless beauty with pale skin and flowing mane of midnight satin, she

Kathryn H. Sargeant   Blood Secrets: The Possession

looked the very picture of the great goddess herself. The flames flickered in her emerald eye, and the ruby lips parted in a warm smile as she motioned them to the cushions across from her. Kaytlin sat as Amee slipped into trance. Focusing on the dancing heart of the sacred flame, Amee lost herself, soaring out of her earthbound body and into the welcoming embrace of time. Stars whirled before her in chaotic ballet and the fates lay before her two different futures to see. One of agony and destruction with a world enslaved by evil: the pain and sadness were too great and she had to turn away. The next held pain and death also but with a glorious rebirth. Four bright stars rebuilding a kingdom lost. The same four stars that jointly held the keys to both salvation and destruction.

"The stars wheel six times. Before the wheel ends the sixth time, you must unite your houses. Four there are and four there need be. Two houses united; two kingdoms to rule. Shadows, uncertainty, a silver star, a wolf, a flame, a tree, these things will play a part. You must act or all will fail. And if you heed me not: Woe unto the world!" Amee swayed and crumpled onto the cushions. Kaytlin leapt to her side.

"Is she..?"

"She will be fine, my lord, but I think it best that you go, now. I will lead you out." She turned and strode grimly through the curtain. The ragged breathing behind told her that they followed and each ringing step sounded in her ears like the knells of doom. She stepped aside and allowed them to pass into the waning sunlight of early evening, offering no explanation for their questioning looks. The only thing she could think to say was simply, "Remember."

10

"It is time for you to come home!" Gregory shouted in exasperation.

After a brief salute, King Duncan had mounted his stallion and galloped back to his waiting retainer, leaving Kaytlin alone with her uncle. Gregory had spent the last eternity trying to cajole the girl and had finally lost his patience in the face of her stoic refusals.

"You belong with your family, in your rightful place as princess, not running around some mountain like a penniless badger!"

"No." she said, simply. He changed tact, trying once more to entice her.

"My dear one, I have a magnificent stallion waiting for you with my retainer. You need not stay forever, just come for a short visit. Meet the family that you don't know. Christopher, and Rose, and Catarine. They are perishing with want, my dear Kaytlin. They want to meet you so badly, to welcome you home. To your mother's home. You know it is what she would have wanted." His voice was gentle and appealing, eroding her will, until he mentioned her mother. Then, his voice changed just slightly, hardening almost imperceptibly. Kaytlin shook her head and stepped away from his outstretched hand.

"If my mother had deemed that a fit life for me, she would have left me there. This is my home, and my life, and Amee needs me. I couldn't begin to learn to be a princess, Uncle. Please understand I am what I am: A priestess of Shondea. Farewell in all your other endeavors." She melted into the shadows of the cave, her eyes stinging with unshed tears.

"So much like your mother." Gregory muttered savagely. He swore, then mounted his horse and galloped away.

Six Years Later

The riders paused atop the hillock and stared down at their destination: Ariangard. The capital city of Zemire was a large sprawling city spilling from the very mouth of the king's favorite castle. Brightly colored banners flew from every window, every rooftop, and merry music floated up to the riders on the hill, yet Blackthorn Castle itself sat like an angry gash in the middle of the valley. Though the high walls were covered in forbidding creeping vine of black thorns that would make scaling difficult for enemies, the large iron bound oak gates were swung wide in welcome. Mikel looked at the yawning maw and shuddered. To him, it looked like the mouth of a demented demon, stretching wide to swallow him whole so the vines could strangle him throughout eternity.

"You look as though you were going to the gallows, brother." Stephen chided good naturedly from beside him.

"I would rather go to the gallows than the chapel, brother. Give me a battlefield any day over a council chamber."

"Then, you picked the wrong order to be born in. Better if you'd been the younger." Stephen's excited stallion danced sideways.

"Had I a choice, I would be no king's son at all. But, don't let anyone hear that from me, or I'll be dubbed the 'poor little princeling'. Well, let's get this last free ride over and done with." Mikel spurred his horse over the ridge and down

13

the paved road that led to Ariangard. "At least they have roads of stone. I'm tired of slogging through mud."

"You complain more than any washerwoman! Do you want all to know you as a bitter, whiny king?" Duncan demanded of his son as he rode up beside him. "You do your family a dishonor, Mikel."

"I am sorry, Father. I will try not to dishonor you any further." Mikel bit each word off viciously. He urged his stallion away.

The entourage rode the rest of the way in silence, winding through streets filled with cheering revelers. Children threw flowers on the street before the horses, and rose petals floated down from open windows above as they made their way to the castle proper. They swung through the open gated arch and into a large courtyard that had been hastily cleared for their arrival. A dais had been erected in its center and atop this dais stood a very beautiful woman in gilt robes. Her long honeyed hair cascaded down her back in a shower of gold, held back from her heart shaped face by a simple diadem. Her brown eyes were as warm and welcoming as the smile that parted her rosy lips.

"Welcome, my lords of Regust. I am Rose, daughter of King Gregory and the princess of Zemire. It is my great privilege to greet you on this fine day. May the Goddess and God smile upon all your endeavors. Our home is your home." She swept her arm around in an all encompassing gesture and the gathered ladies and knights cheered.

"Most gracious and beautiful lady may the stars shine forever on you and yours. We are honored to accept your hospitality and good will and return them

14

a thousand fold." King Duncan touched his fingers to his lips and flipped them toward her, as if launching his kiss to the air. He and the wedding party dismounted. Rose fairly floated down the steps of the dais to the king's side and gazed up at him with warm but troubled eyes.

"My father sends his regrets for not welcoming you himself. A messenger came scant hours before you and the news was wretched. My father sits in counsel, now, over the matter. I was told to bring you to his chambers as soon as you arrived. Please, follow me." She turned, leading them through an arched doorway formed by two carven trees, their branches intertwining to close the top. The passageways were long and winding, yet warm as they passed through; torches lit the way at three-foot intervals and danced coy lightning over suits of armor and rich tapestries. Mikel admired the polished steel as they strode swiftly by, and was impressed that such a small and dainty appearing creature as the princess could set such a swift pace. The girl didn't seem to be put out by the speed at all; indeed she was hardly winded. But…no. He shook his head. That wasn't the same suit of armor that they had passed before.

"Tell me, Rose, did you hear the messengers' news?" Duncan asked as they turned down another passage. Mikel surmised they must be going to the king's private chambers for no throne room would be so deep inside a castle.

"I did. News has come from Silver Wood: ferocious creatures have attacked the Amazons there. No two descriptions are the same. The only thing that is known for sure is that the Amazon queen, Linara, has been gravely wounded. Her daughters do not think she will survive much longer, and are beseeching my father for aide." They walked in silence for a while, until she finally stopped outside a large iron bound door. She knocked once, then swung the door open and gestured her guests inside. Gregory rose from behind a desk strewn with maps and papers to clasp each of their hands in turn.

"Apparently, the peoples of Silver Wood recon time differently than we do. I am afraid it begins," he said, grimly.

Rose paused outside the ebony double doors. The torchlight danced over the carvings of mythical beasts upon them, giving them eerie life. That was one thing that she did not share with her dear sister: A belief in magic and myths. If she could not see it, or touch it, or taste it, then it was not real. As she raised her hand to knock, the doors swung silently inward. The woman before her was dressed in tunic and breeches, a long sword belted at her side. Her long black braids were tipped in small metal stars and brown eyes gazed placidly out from under dark eyelashes. The pale skin of her face glowed in the torchlight as she stepped back to let Rose enter. A smile of exquisite pearl formed on her face as she clapped her friend on the back.

"Greetings, Rose. Fair speech you gave." Lorell said, closing the door behind her.

"I thought I saw you on the wall, but you disappeared before I was sure."

"Aye, Catarine wanted me to give her an account of the princes' arrival." A sudden crash brought Lorell's sword from its' scabbard like a striking viper and

Kathryn H. Sargeant   Blood Secrets: The Possession

the mercenary to a defensive position before Rose. The maid who had dropped the crystal vase screamed and ran from the room, disappearing behind silken curtains. With a snort, Lorell replaced her blade and turned back to Rose, who was replacing the small dagger she had drawn from her sash.

"Will I ever be as quick as you?" Rose asked, softly. The young mercenary smiled, reassuringly.

"When you have had more practice, although with your new duties I don't know when you'll find the time."

"I hate this! I would rather run away and join a mercenary band or pirates! Let's go, Lorell! Let's leave this place and all its trappings far behind." Rose grabbed the other girls sleeve in a passion. Lorell looked into her eyes for a long moment and then shook her head, sadly.

"You would be miserable, Rose. Your sense of duty and honor would hound you to an early grave. Try not to think of your marriage as a sentence, but as an adventure." Lorell advised. Rose snorted.

"Why don't you take up that adventure?"

"Are you insane? And sentence myself to a life of dresses and cookery? Gods!" Lorell rolled her eyes and laughter rang out from the other side of the room. They turned. Catarine stood by the curtains that separated her bedchamber from the sitting area.

"I don't think that's the way to encourage her, Lorell," she said, tossing back her wet ringlets. "It won't be so bad, Rose. I hear that both princes are handsome."

Kathryn H. Sargeant   Blood Secrets: The Possession

"Aye, that they are. And Mikel does have an air about him that makes my head swim. I got lost twice on the way to father's study because of his mere presence. I am so glad they did not notice." Rose blushed.

"I believe she has succumbed to her fate in the most heinous of ways." Lorell said in a morose tone and shuddered. "She has fallen in love."

"Oh, Shondea, no!" Catarine gasped in mock horror. "Come, Rose, help me dress. I need your expertise."

Christopher sat alone at the small table, staring morosely at the small ball of glass nestled among the folds of the blue silk draping. The size of a hen, it stared back at him, cold, uncaring, and empty. Why wouldn't it work? He took a deep breath, cleared his mind, and tried to let the image form.

Nothing.

It worked for Catarine, why shouldn't it work for him? Perhaps the image he sought was too old. She would be a young woman, now, not the babe he remembered. Her hair would be long and luscious, not wispy and thin. Her eyes would still be blue as the sky, he'd bet his life on that. But what about the rest?

"Oh, cousin, if only you would come home," he sighed to the dark room. His fist slammed down on the table. He had decided. Once this whole wedding thing was over, he would go to the oracle and see her. See for himself what she had become, and maybe even reclaim the heart she had stolen. "I come, Kaytlin."

He went to tell his father of his decision.

On the table, the glass started to glow, softly. It filled with a swirling smoke as dark and thick as summer twilight. The mists parted slowly, and the glow brightened. Inside the silent crystal a battle raged: Lizard like man creatures swarmed over the walls of Blackthorn Castle while the garrison fought to repel them. The door to the castle exploded outward in a shower of sparks and splinters and a figure stepped out carrying a slumped form. It wore the garb of a prince of Regust....

"..with my blessing, Christopher. Perhaps you will have better luck than I." Gregory paced in front of the fire, hands clasped firmly behind his back. He stole a sidelong glance at his son from under lowered brows. Christopher sat rigidly in the high backed chair, his eyes following the dance of the flames beyond his father. The light from the flames tinted his blonde hair a blood red that seemed to pool down into his eyes. Gregory shook himself. "Well, I am off to the feasting hall. Go fetch your sisters. They will no doubt want to make a grand entrance." Christopher nodded, dutifully, and left as quietly as he had come. Gregory felt a twinge of regret as he watched his son go. He should have been king, should have been furious at the circumstances, but he simply accepted it. He would do what he felt must be done and not complain, like his mother before him: Or his aunt. Gregory snatched a goblet from the table and hurled it into the flames.

Mikel glared at the clothing that lay on his bed. The tunic was fine crushed velvet, black with gold trim. The breeches were the softest leather, dyed black as night with gold lacings. The colors of home, the colors of the Regustian flag. Against his tan skin and dark hair they would make him look like a demon knight. It was a look he cultivated. Stephen would no doubt opt for blue, to showcase his blonde hair and blue eyes. Each to his own strengths and looks. Stephen never missed an opportunity to capitalize on looking like his mother. Indeed, little brother never missed any opportunity because he was special. Mother's special little princeling…. A knock on the door snapped his angry train of thought.

"Enter." He called, picking up the breeches. A discreet cough behind him made him turn. Rose stood leaning against the door, her eyes roaming shamelessly over his naked body, her lips parting in a seductive smile.

"My, my, but I think I've the better end of the deal for once in my life." She drifted across the room to run a finger lightly over his chest. His hands rose to her silken hair and he pulled her against him.

"You shouldn't be here, princess," he whispered hoarsely and she laughed softly against his neck.

"Why not? We are to be married, after all." Rose lifted herself onto her tiptoes and planted her delicate lips against his mouth. Soft at first, the kiss soon grew demanding and Mikel felt his body start to respond to her. He crushed her

21

against him, his hand traveling her back, tangling in her hair. Mikel turned her until she was against the bed and she pulled him down with her...

Christopher opened the door to Catarine's room and walked inside.

"I've news, little sparrow. Come out from your nest and hear it," he called, playfully. She came out from behind the curtains, adjusting a small silver and sapphire crown atop her head. "You look magnificent." Her gown was royal blue silk with white ribbons adorning the bodice and tying the waist. It flowed like water down her, teasingly, to brush the floor in a whispering kiss. Her hair was loose and flowing, waves of harvest gold to her waist. And, glinting from her exposed neck, a simple sapphire tear dangled in the hollow of her throat.

"Where is Rose? She should have been back by now. Why, Christopher, you are positively glowing! What has happened?" she demanded.

"I've decided to go to Caladren Mountain and bring Kaytlin back myself. I think she will come if I ask her. Either way, I will see her and find out once and for all...."

"If she could love you in return? Oh, Christopher, that is wonderful!! Perhaps we will have a second wedding to celebrate!" She threw herself into his embrace. "I do wonder what is keeping Rose. She will be so happy to hear this!"

Rose sat astride Mikel, gazing down at the satisfied sleepy smile on his face. She idly traced his shoulder bone to the hollow of his neck, then bent down to give his chin a playful nip.

"By far the better end of the deal." she murmured against his cheek, spilling little kisses across his face. She raised herself just a little to look into his languid eyes. Mikel stiffened. The burning coals of her eyes seared into his; she hissed and a forked tongue darted out to taste his lips. Mikel tried to sit up, to throw her off, but her fingers dug like talons into his shoulders and he could not move her. A vice closed around his heart, squeezing the breath from his lungs as he struggled to scream. She leered. "Now, little princeling, we've both had our fun. It's time to work. Our master grows impatient."

"Take her with you." the woman said softly, her opaque eyes searching his face.

"I will." he vowed, kissing her hand. He rose to leave the chamber.

"Take good care of her, my king." The ground pitched beneath his feet and the walls around him started to crumble. The passageway behind him filled with stone and dust. He ran. A man appeared before him, holding back a struggling girl. Together they raced down the corridor as it tried to swallow them and out into the blazing midday sun. The man turned green eyes to him, auburn

hair askew. The gauntlet had been torn from his left arm and a star shone there. A star to match the one on her bare shoulder.

"King Stephen, are you injured?"

Stephen started awake. In the deepening twilight, the room was sickeningly unfamiliar. After a moment he remembered where he was but even as he dressed for dinner, those green eyes haunted him. And the words: what could they mean?

Rose stepped into the corridor from her room and started back to Catarine's. She had changed into a simple gown of soft violet with a gold embroidered bodice over the top. Her hair had been twisted up into a snood of braided gold mesh and the cloth of gold slippers adorning her feet made her footing treacherous on the worn stone of the castle floor. She sped her pace, turning down another corridor. They would be waiting for her and she did not want to be late. Suddenly, her foot slid out from under her and she threw herself forward in an attempt not to fall. From behind, an arm slid protectively around her waist and set her back on her feet. She turned.

"You weren't injured, were you, Rose?" Mikel asked gruffly. His eyes searched her for any obvious sign but found none.

"Only my pride. I thought I was more graceful than that." she laughed shakily. Something about him made her uneasy. It wasn't just that he looked like a demon prince in his attire or that she would soon be this stranger's wife. There was something about his eyes, something that wasn't there before....

"You are graceful, never fear of that. Besides, I am known for my unfailing sense of direction and I am lost."

"Then, I will make you a pact. I won't tell anyone you got lost if you don't tell anyone about my slip." she smiled uneasily, stepping back unconsciously from his leonine smile. She hadn't noticed that before. Perhaps, she had been smitten at first and was just unwilling to notice his flaws. He reached out and took her hand in his clammy one.

"It is a deal, fair one. We shall say we were simply walking and lost track of the time. Shall we?" he started walking, carrying her along with him.

"I must go to my sister's chamber and collect her. It will only take a moment, then we can all go to the hall." Rose took the lead, wracking her brain for a polite way to pull her hand free and finding none. His skin was so cold, so damp. She hoped it was only nerves or this marriage would indeed be an 'adventure' of the worst kind for her.

The door to Catarine's chamber stood slightly ajar and they could hear voices from inside as they approached. Rose stopped just inside the doorway, Mikel at her side, and clapped a hand to her mouth to stifle a laugh. Christopher and Catarine sat across from each other at a small table, both squinting at the

25

brightly colored cards they each held. Christopher shuffled and reshuffled his hand as Catarine hummed slightly. Suddenly, Catarine let a tremendous whoop and slapped her cards onto the table.

"Haygon! I win!"

"You cheat!" Christopher quipped, tossing his hand face down on the tabletop.

"No I don't, you just can't deal."

"Not when you stack the deck."

"You both cheat and you do it badly!" Rose jeered from the door.

"No we don't!" they cried in unison, turning to her. The laughter died on their faces.

"This is Mikel, Prince of Regust. Mikel, this is my sister and brother, Catarine and Christopher." Catarine blushed hotly and Christopher ran a self-conscious hand through his blonde curls as they both rose. Mikel clasped Christopher's hand and bowed to Catarine, who curtsied in return. She suddenly felt light headed and her insides began to shriek in cold dread. There was something not right here.

"Shall we?" Christopher asked, offering her his arm. Catarine shook herself and smiled.

"Oh, yes! I am so looking forward to meeting your father and brother, Mikel."

"You are in for quite a treat, Catarine." Mikel assured her and Rose shivered.

Kathryn H. Sargeant

Stephen stole another sidelong glance at Catarine and was amazed, again. How could no one else see it? She fairly glowed with an inner light that suffused her face with a heavenly glow. His heart swelled at the thought of their marriage. He had known from the moment she had entered the room behind his brother that he would love no other woman until the day he died. He lost track of the conversation, so her laugh took him by surprise. Catarine pushed herself back from the table, her eyes catching Stephen's as she rose.

"If you will excuse me, I feel the need for fresh air. Perhaps, Stephen, you would care to join me?" she asked, lightly.

"It would be a pleasure, my lady," he rose and followed her as she passed through one of the many tapestries hanging along the wall. To his surprise, it opened into a lush garden full of blooming night flowers and soft perfume. The moon perched atop the garden wall, full and round, casting a bright and bluish light upon the large stately oak that sat like a king in the middle of the garden.

"This is where we would play as children. I still love to come here. Over past the tree is a door that will take you outside the castle. It was put there as an escape route by my great grandfather when he first built Blackthorn. I think it is covered over by vines, now, though. Anyway, with our kingdom at peace, we will not need escape routes." she chattered amiably as they walked the crushed shell path to the tree. From its great branches hung a set of swings and Catarine settled upon one of them. "I love this place so."

Kathryn H. Sargeant   Blood Secrets: The Possession

"Then, we shall have to stay here and let Mikel and Rose take our home in Regust." Stephen said decisively, pushing her gently. Mischief overcame him, and in seconds he had her soaring into the sky, her hair streaming and her laughter ringing out across the garden.

"Join me, Stephen!" she called on an upward swing and he darted out of her way.

"Alright, I believe I will." The diamond chips littering the heavens gazed down at the two of them as they strove reach the sky in their limited flight. Taken with the mortals' game, they bent low and then pulled away each time one reached forward to pluck them from the sky. Amid the warm companionship and laughter, a cold wind touched the back of Catarine's neck and she leaned back in her swing. Movement in the tree branches overhead near the ropes of Stephen's swing caught her eye. The rope snapped and sent Stephen sailing through the air and into one of the rose bushes. Catarine leapt from her swing, landing like a cat and raced to the spot where he had disappeared.

"Stephen?" she called. "Stephen, are you injured? Stephen, speak to me!" With a moan, Stephen crawled from the bushes and collapsed, bruised and bleeding, at her feet. "Oh, Stephen, let me help you."

"I'm alright, Catarine. Just a little scratched. I didn't mean to alarm you," he said nonchalantly. She bent and slid an arm underneath his shoulders and helped him up.

"I'm taking you back to my room and I'm calling for a physician. Those thorns could be poisonous. Some here are."

Lorell entered the brightly lit room and smiled reassuringly at the worried girl pacing its length.

"You need not worry, Catarine; he's going to be fine. Just a little sore."

"It's not that, Lorell. Just before the ropes broke, I saw something in the tree. I just can't shake the feeling that that was no accident. Someone wanted Stephen to get hurt, maybe killed." Catarine ran a hand through her disheveled hair and looked around nervously.

"Calm yourself, Catarine. I will speak to the guard captain and have extra lookouts posted. And I will check that swing rope myself, as soon as there is light enough to see properly." Lorell took her by the arm and guided her to the bed. She settled the princess into the soft silken folds of the blankets and squeezed her hand. "It will all be fine."

"I'm not sure, Lorell. This feels strange. Something is terribly wrong."

"I know, Catarine. I feel it, too, but I promise you everything will work out for the best. Now, get some rest. Jerusha and Breandis are right outside, and I am going to speak to the guards now. Rest." Lorell brushed her fingers over Catarine's eyes, forcing the lids closed, then moved out to the sitting area. The two warrior women stood on either side of the door, waiting. "Guard her well. This feels like the calm before the storm to me. I'll be back soon. Let no one near Catarine until I return."

Deep inside Caladren Mountain, Kaytlin woke with a scream. The room spun crazily around her and she felt the bed tilt beneath her as if the whole mountain were sliding. A stinging slap cracked across her face like lightning and the sharp pain brought everything back into focus. Amee sat beside her on the twisted sweat soaked sheets, gripping her shoulders.

"Kaytlin, child, you were screaming! What is it? What did you see?" her voice was strident with fear.

"It is too late! It is too late, Amee! It is loose and it will destroy us all. They did not listen! They did not listen!" Kaytlin sobbed roughly. She shuddered once and then collapsed back onto the bed in a deep slumber: The exhausted slumber of a first *sight*.

In the corridor, a shadow detached from the curve of the wall, slipping quickly into another recess. Drawn by the screams, it waited for Amee to leave and then slipped inside to stare down at the sleeping girl. It was not yet time.

Flames. She was the flame, dancing across the wood, leaping from a knot to spark the very air. She floated on a current of air, borne up one of the many air tubes cut into the mountain and into the darkness. She danced on the velvet of the night, rising higher into the sky until the very stars absorbed her. Icy cold gripped her as she became one with the mother, gazing down coldly upon a world that meant nothing yet everything to her. In the East, the sky was filled

32

with laughter and music and a warm glowing light. Wedding banners flew, and cooks prepared feasts like the world had never seen. But, a dark spot moved about the light, flitting hither and thither, almost too fast to perceive.

A roaring crash split the air to the West. A mountain collapsed and from its rubble a spired castle rose. Black as the heart of hell, it stabbed into the sky, planting its evil roots deep into the ground. Monsters poured from its yawning gates, and laughter so grim and evil that it made even the stars quake rolled from its foundations. Amee watched in horror as the army swarmed over the remaining mountains and into Silver Wood, driving all before it, killing mercilessly and wantonly. There was no escape. The souls of creatures caught unawares floated upward to join the great mother. There were so many! Amee heard a desperate cry from the East, and turned to see the light being devoured by darkness from inside.

"Gaze on me, whore of Shondea! Gaze on the new lord and master of all! Your demon charge will be one of my concubines and you will see no more!" The roaring laugh smashed the night sky like an angry fist, sending shards of blackness spiraling through the air. Amee turned once more to the West.

Above the castle rose a monstrous form: It gnashed razor fangs at her in a demonic smile, dripping putrid ooze from cracked lips. The leathery skin was a dark green, stretched taught across a skeletal face of reptilian nature. Yellow eyes burned maliciously at her, and the ridged spine that ran from mid forehead to the tip of his long tail quivered as he laughed. Four muscular arms reached for

Kathryn H. Sargeant   Blood Secrets: The Possession

her, each ending in a powerful talon, and it raised huge thighs to plant clawed feet on the mountains surrounding him.

"I will rule forever." The creature began to shimmer, the very air around it to bleed. In the glowing bright darkness, the creature began to transform into something human. A tall young man with shoulder length black hair and dark eyes, his face hidden by a beard that traced cheekbones and jaw line, but filled no further. A young man who could pass easily for a prince of Hell, itself: Mikel. The darkness exploded in a sound and fury of universes colliding, sending shards of evil flying into the galaxy. Amee threw her arm over her face an instant too late. Slivers pierced her eyes and exploded, robbing her of her sight.

Amee collapsed back into the cushions and was still.

Dornan stomped through the garden, anger bubbling in his chest. It was bad enough that the little twit had been chosen as the princess's personal guard, now the arrogant little witch had the nerve to tell him how to run a watch!?! Who did she think she was? Of course, she did it so politely.

"Would you please humor me? Just for tonight? It would ease Catarine's mind. We would both consider it a personal favor." Lorell had said. What could he say? She had invoked the princess's name. He couldn't very well tell the princess to go get stuffed, now could he? Dornan couldn't wait for the day

Stephen decided to put that upstart in her place, put her back in charge of the nursery and the kitchen where all women belonged. He and that Mikel would have enough good male soldiers to make her and her two companions unnecessary, to say the least. He snorted to himself. Maybe one of them would decide to take her to hand, teach her the pleasures of being what she was: A pretty woman. Maybe, it would even be him.

He passed by the overgrown door to the outside without noticing and continued on with his rounds. He hailed three other guards as he passed and then went back into the dining hall. A quick cup of mead wouldn't hurt anyone, least of all him. He would roust out some more guards later.

A yellow fog poured through the streets of Ariangard, clinging like a living thing to all that it touched, slithering ever closer to the castle. It pooled alongside the thorn-draped walls like a tide, crashing back on itself in swirling eddies where the stone rebuffed it. It began to pulse with a sickly green light.

A creature began to rise from the mists.

The oval head was elongated to a point on the crown, the face hard and flat. A sharp, beak-like nose jutted from its center to hang over clacking, crab-like jaws. Long fangs curved downward from blackened, leathery lips to drip venom into the crawling mist below it. A large, barrel shaped chest followed, along with powerfully muscled arms and legs, all covered in gray armored scales. The demon opened its' glowing white eyes and growled. More of them came out of the mists around him. Digging their talons into the thorns, they quickly swarmed over the top of the wall and disappeared into the gardens shadows.

"I tell you, Joseph, she had the biggest jugs you ever saw, and a face of an angel. And what that girl could do..." the two guards passed within inches of the horde, unseeing. The first wave advanced slowly as more creatures crept over the walls.

Kathryn H. Sargeant   Blood Secrets: The Possession

Mikel prowled restlessly down the hall, shadows rippling behind him. There. He kicked the center of the double doors and they burst open, sending chambermaids screaming. Rose rolled from the bed, pulling the sword clumsily from the scabbard hanging on the bedpost. She stood confused for a moment, staring at him in incomprehension. Warriors filled the room behind him. Rose let out a small cry and charged, bringing her sword down in a life-ending chop....

He caught the blade between his hands and wrenched it from her. He tossed it carelessly aside and seized her roughly by the arms.

"That's not very nice, Rose. What happened to your home is my home?" he sneered. She screamed as he slung her against the wall, and darkness claimed her.

Alarm bells rang throughout the castle and the corridors echoed with screams. Catarine bolted from the bed.

"Lorell? Lorell, what's happening?" she cried. Lorell stood at the open doorway watching the halls.

"I don't know, Catarine. What's this? Mikel is coming, he can tell us." Lorell gasped and slammed the door, ramming the iron bar home. She ran halfway across the room and whirled to face the door, blade drawn. "He comes with an army at his back! Ready yourselves, Catarine get back there!" The doors exploded in a shower of splinter and sparks and Lorell leapt forward, sword raised to meet the rush. Mikel stepped calmly through the broken doors, looking around at the wreckage with mild contempt.

"You start a war with your actions, Prince. Leave now, and I will let you live." Lorell snarled.

"You'd be so kind? Then, perhaps, I'll let you live as well." Mikel twitched his fingers and the army charged through the doors, blades flashing in the torchlight. Lorell's own blade flashed like lightning as she met the charge, blocking one thrust while sidestepping another. She whipped her head sideways, using her braids as a whip to wrench the blade from yet another's scabbed claws. A battle cry tore from her lips as she kicked the feet out from under one of her foes, and she flicked a throwing star from her gauntlet and snapped it into the eye of another. Acid streamed down its face and it howled in agony, stumbling into the path of a slashing sword. Sounds of fighting behind her assured her that Breandis and Jerusha were still alive and a rush of pride swelled her for a moment: they had not broken in the face of the enemy. Lorell sliced through the neck of one foe even as she flicked a star into another eye. The air behind her vibrated and she hit the ground, rolling to her feet and turning in one smooth movement. She brought her sword up under the ribcage of the creature as its wild swing passed through the space where her neck had just been.

Kathryn H. Sargeant   Blood Secrets: The Possession

"ENOUGH!" Mikel roared and the horde disengaged, moving warily back to their master's side. Mikel smiled appreciatively at Lorell, raising an inquisitive eyebrow. "Impressive. I could use a force such as you in my army. Join me."

"I would die first." Lorell spat. She charged, blade poised for the kill. Mikel's hand flashed upward and her blade shattered. She dropped to the floor, rolling toward one of the fallen swords littering the floor and came to her feet with a snarl. She faced Mikel. He shook his head, regretfully, and pointed at her. Smoke issued from his fingertip, an ebony snake that lashed around her neck and began to squeeze. Lorell dropped to her knees, digging at her throat, trying to pull the snake free.

"Very impressive. And such loyalty. Kill the others, bring me the princess." he ordered. The demons swarmed forward in a wave so thick that there was no room to move and when that wave rolled back seconds later, it was over. Jerusha and Breandis lay like broken dolls upon the floor and a screaming Catarine was being drug toward Mikel by a large demon. Its skin was ebony and hard muscled, with long white hair that reached the small of its' back. It could have been a man, had it been colored differently. "Continue your assault, Torq, but leave that girl unharmed. I almost respect her."

The demon passed Catarine into Mikel's arms and motioned his creatures out the door. Mikel held Catarine close, staring into her eyes. "Sleep." He hissed. Catarine collapsed against him, unconscious, and he lifted her into his arms.

Christopher swung his blade like a berserker, slashing foe after foe as he cut his way toward his sisters' rooms. He had to get to them, to protect them. He stumbled over a corpse and fell to his knees, dropping his sword. The last sight he ever saw was Gregory's sightless eyes staring up at nothing.

Kaytlin shivered. She turned behind a tree and waited. Nothing. No sound, no stir of air, no scent, nothing.

"Pull yourself together, girl. Amee needs meat." She scolded herself softly, pushing away from the tree. She set an arrow across her bow and continued on. The worn wood in her palm eased her and the waning sun cast dappled shadows around her. She breathed deeply of the rich green scented air and cocked her head to listen. Slight rustling up ahead. Kaytlin crept forward, bow drawn. Whatever was ahead, it was hers. She inched cautiously though the underbrush until she could see it: A beautiful doe stood off to her right, grazing on large tufts of sweet grass, it's soft fur rippling over tender muscles as it lazily munched away. Kaytlin drifted her bow to the right. The doe sensed movement and brought up its' head. The arrow flew true. The doe hit the ground with a heavy thump, the fletching of the arrow sticking from one liquid brown eye. Kaytlin slung the doe up onto her shoulders and headed for home.

In the trees above her, something stirred, slipping from branch to branch. It followed her closely, always.

Kaytlin turned away from the mountain, heading not toward home but to an older, darker part of the forest. Tree branches interwove above her head like a canopy and the trunks of the trees grew thicker and more closely together. She hummed as she walked, her fingers idly stroking the dagger at her side, going through the consecrating motions unconsciously. Shondea would be well pleased by the offering.

"Kaytlin, is that you?" Amee called uncertainly from beside the fire.

"Yes. I brought venison." Kaytlin dropped the rolled skin from her shoulders, untied the ends and unrolled it. She spitted several pieces and set them to hang over the fire. Amee looked frail in the dancing light, her pale skin even paler now, her hair limp. She looked lost and young and broken. Kaytlin cleared a lump from her throat. "You should rest, Amee. This damp air is not good for you. There is an unseasonable chill tonight."

"It follows you." Amee said simply. A hungry whining bark came from the bushes. Kaytlin hurried to toss one of the seared meat pieces in that direction.

Amee chuckled. "My dear, soft hearted one. Will you feed every creature in the woods before yourself?"

"At least you. Here, just the way you like it." They ate in silence, chewing contentedly by the fire. "Amee? I had a dream last night."

"Oh?" Amee set the stick aside and folded her hands in her lap. Kaytlin hesitated for a moment. "Go on."

"There was a horrible storm raging around me, tearing at me like claws. I was trying to stand on a rock or boulder of some kind. My insides felt like I had swallowed live coals and there was a man holding my left hand. We were desperate for a third person to get up on the rocks with us but the storm kept driving him back. I was very scared. I held out my hand and screamed his name. Then, I woke up." Kaytlin shrugged. She rose, suddenly, and began to pace.

"What did he look like?" Amee asked.

"Tall, very tall, taller than Uncle Gregory. Wavy auburn hair. His eyes were green as new leaves. He was very handsome, lean and well built. A warrior. Jason. That's what I screamed. Jason. He seemed so familiar to me. Am I going insane?" she asked, and Amee chuckled.

"The question all seers ask of themselves. The answer is usually no. Your destiny calls, Kaytlin. It tells you that whether you go East or West, North or South, or stay right here, it will catch you. This is something you were meant to do." Amee cautioned.

"And if I choose not to? Life can't make me do anything I don't want to."

"Can't it? I did not raise a fool. You will fulfill your destiny, child, to whichever end you may." Amee rose to her feet. "Sleep on it, Kaytlin, and give me your answer tomorrow." Kaytlin watched her disappear into the mountain and then threw herself onto the ground.

"I will not leave you, Amee. No matter what. This is my home and I will stay here and defend it. And you."

The wolf howled once from the brush.

Lorell staggered from the room, coughing roughly, sword in each hand. Taken from the bloodied hands of her fallen comrades, they gleamed hungrily in the torchlight, screaming for vengeance as she hacked and slashed her way through the melee. She had to catch Mikel, had to save Catarine somehow. A knot of warriors hove into view, backing some other warrior into a corner. Lorell charged, slicing through the group like a scythe through ripened wheat. Stephen finished the last one off as she turned to see who she had saved. For a moment, their eyes locked. For a moment, Lorell considered plunging her sword through his chest.

"Mikel has Catarine." she said and relief flooded his face. "He is the leader of this army." They swept down the corridor toward the courtyard, powered by anger and blood lust. Stephen slipped in a pool of blood, landing heavily on top of a cluster of corpses. Agonized wails tore open his throat.

"Get up! Get up! Your father is dead, get up unless you wish to join him!" Lorell jerked him to his feet. Stephen shook her off.

"Get me to my brother." he snarled. Drenched in gore, the smell of blood and death in their nostrils, they charged through the doorway into the courtyard. The fighting was frenetic; each demon that was cut down became two more. Stephen raced up the dais that Rose had greeted them from and searched the blood soaked arena. Mikel sat on a large black stallion in the gateway, smiling in cool disdain over the fighting. He winked at Stephen. Catarine pulled at the ropes binding her to the saddle in front of Mikel and he pulled her head around and kissed her savagely. Mikel whirled his steed and sped through the gate, followed by an ebony giant holding Rose tightly to its chest.

"I'll come for you, Mikel!" Stephen shouted, raising his sword high in the air. "By the shining stars, you will pay for what you have done!" The castle rocked, and fissures cracked open the ground, swallowing demons and soldiers, alike. Stephen pitched from the dais and rolled as the panicked people surged toward the castle door.

"Run for the gates! Get outside!" Lorell shouted above the din, turning people around. She pushed them toward the open gate as the walls started to crumble. Lorell leaped over a flaming fissure and knocked Stephen out of the way of a falling archway. The stone tumbled onto her, pinning her leg. Stephen grabbed a couple of guards that were racing by, and the three of them managed to heave the stone up and pull her out. Stephen threw her over his shoulder and raced for the collapsing gate.

"No, I don't want to see!" Kaytlin curled into a ball on her bed, rocking back and forth. Terror drenched her in cold sweat as the pictures kept flashing before her eyes in sickening succession: A castle crumbling, stones crushing children as they ran for safety. A blood drenched girl pinned beneath a large stone. Gregory sprawled in his own blood, eyes unseeing as the castle crashed down upon him. A girl's face swirled before her. Honey blonde hair, hazel eyes, her full lips trembled as she mouthed the words 'Help me!' The name Catarine exploded inside Kaytlin's head, driving spikes through her brain, and bile rose to her throat. Convulsions wracked her body: the smell of sulfur and sweaty horses pummeled her; hot acrid winds ripped at her; she was being carried away. "Demon-steeds." she moaned, rolling to the edge of the bed. She vomited.

Kaytlin dove into the cold water of the lagoon, dragging herself as far along the bottom as she could before bursting through the rainbow hued surface. The waterfall rumbled comfortably across the way and the sound was soothing. Her trembling muscles eased in the water's embrace and she floated on her back in the moonlight. A breeze rippled the surface and chilled her skin, so she dove again into the depths, making faces at the fish she chanced across. She came up laughing and tossed a handful of water into the air, dancing beneath the droplets. Humming wordlessly, she struck out for shore and stretched out on the soft moss to lay in the moonlight. She fell asleep.

Above, the shadow settled down to watch.

Blackthorn Castle had become a twisted behemoth, spewing forth rubble and human debris. Ariangard lay in ruins. Stephen looked out over the devastation from under the healer's pavilion. So many dead, so many lost. Why? He turned his back on the carnage. The ground around him was littered with makeshift pallets. Wounded stretched as far back as he could see, flies buzzing around them as they moaned. Priests moved silently, giving blessings and comfort where they may. Stephen stopped one, asked a question. The priest frowned, then pointed down the row and moved on. Stephen carefully made his way down the narrow aisle, stopping to lend a word of encouragement or praise where he could, until he came to the pallet he sought. The girl was deathly pale, her eyes closed, hands folded over her chest. His stomach twisted. Was he too late?

"Lorell." he said, softly. She stirred, eyes fluttering open. Lorell smiled through pain-clouded eyes.

"You look awful." she whispered hoarsely, and started to cough. Stephen eased her into a sitting position and helped her sip some water.

"You should see yourself, my friend. You were amazing, Lorell. I've never seen anyone, let alone a woman, fight as you did." Stephen helped her to lie back down, and then took her hand in his. "You saved my life and countless others. I would give anything if you were well enough to ride with me, now. I am sorry that it was my flesh that brought us all to this."

"Stephen, is your brother a wizard?"

"No."

"Then, he is possessed. He used sorcery against me in Catarine's chamber."

"Then, I will need magic of my own to fight against whatever has him."

"Go to Caladren. If the Oracle can't give you something, maybe she can tell you where to get it." Lorell started to cough, again, and it was a good while before she could speak. Stephen sat numbly, watching as two priests heaved a body between them and carried it out. Another moaning figure swathed in bandages took its' place. "Stephen?"

"I don't know what to do. There is so much," he trailed off, his voice hollow with despair. He sat for a moment longer. When he spoke next, it was with a firm and commanding voice. "Lorell, I will go to Caladren and on to save my queen. You are hereby charged with the duty of organizing our people and rebuilding our city."

"Stephen, they will not listen to me."

"They will or by Shondea I will string them up by their toes! You are my viceroy, from now until I return. And if I do not return, you will be queen. Rest, Lorell. I will see to it." Stephen went in search of a scribe.

Mikel skirted the sacred mountain. He would deal with them later. Now, he was growing weary and he needed to rest. The possession was not complete and the spell he had cast over the girls was tiring his new flesh. The steeds rode at a Hell's pace, their hooves striking sparks off the air as they raced two inches off the ground. His captives were content to watch the scenery fly by. Now, they were docile little lambs but let his attention waver and they would become wildcats, again. With a mighty leap, the demon steeds cleared the deadly Plains of Corwith and landed on the edges of Silver Wood. Mikel ran a hand through his sweat-drenched hair. The boy was fighting, again; he could feel the grip he had slipping.

"Master, the bridge." Torq hissed from behind him. They had reached a circle of large stones. Mikel stretched forth his hand and a rainbow of shadow hues spun from the center of the circle. The tree branches above drew backward as it shot upwards and across the remaining forest and over the mountain range. They urged their steeds onto the shadow road and came down over the mountain to the very door of Nepanthier. Mikel dismounted, tiredly.

"See them to their rooms. I must rest," he mumbled, staggering into the open doorway. As soon as he was out of sight, the spell broke. Rose and Catarine began to scream, kicking and scratching anything that came in contact with them. Torq plucked them from the saddles and carried them, one under each giant arm, through the yawning maw that served as the castle's main entrance.

Stephen rode out the next morning. The delay did not make him happy, but there had been things to do before he could go, and the gathering of horses and supplies and uninjured men took longer than he had hoped. No one had fought him on Lorell. For that he was eternally grateful to the Fates. But even as they smiled, it seemed, they cut his feet out from under him. Only twenty men were fit to ride. Twenty-one against a horde. And of those, only four were from his own retainer: Matthew, his brother Maden, Kraig, and Palon. Only Kraig and

Palon were well known to him, friends from boyhood. The other two were hire swords that his father had taken on earlier in the year.

They rode hard, eating in the saddle and catching naps as they could. Stephen rode at the head, leading the way while the other three Regustians took up point and rearguard positions. They did not stop for rest. Each man burned with a desire for revenge. They must save their precious princesses. No matter what the cost.

Stephen saw him first. He sat on a shadow dappled pony just inside the tree line, watching the party ride closer. The man did not seem surprised to see them; indeed he seemed to wait for them. Stephen signaled a halt, and then slowly walked his lathered stallion forward. The man walked his pony forward into the sunlight. Auburn hair pulled back from his smooth face and green eyes appraised Stephen coolly. Muscles rippled across his chest and arms as the man saluted.

"Hail, King Stephen. I come to join your quest. Do you know me?" he asked. Stephen frowned.

"Aye. From dreams. But how do I know you to be friend and not foe?" Stephen demanded. The man unbuckled his left gauntlet, and held up his arm. In the center of his wrist a blue star blazed with unnatural light.

"I dare say you not only recognize this sign but bear the same somewhere. My name is Jason, and what part I play in your puzzle I do not know. But, somehow, I am part of your quest. Will you allow me to help?" Jason asked grimly. Stephen lightly fingered his thigh. His own star mark burned there.

"Come, brother. We have a lot to talk about and a long way to go before we may rest. Let's start with the dreams."

They dismounted in the clearing outside the cave's mouth. The petitioner's bell had been removed from the tripod next to the cave and the

Kathryn H. Sargeant   Blood Secrets: The Possession

torches had been put out. There was no sound from woods or empty hole. Stephen shuddered. It was as if the place were.....dead. Matthew sauntered over to the cave and poked his head into the darkness. Three arrows whizzed from the trees, pinning his jerkin to the wooden tripod in rapid succession. He leapt back, ripping the leather and landing in a sprawled heap on the ground seconds before a rock the size of a hen's egg came shooting toward his head. With a fierce ululating cry, Kaytlin leapt into the clearing, the setting sun glancing off her blade to flash crimson into the eyes of the party.

"Who dares disturb the rest of Amee, priestess of Shondea?" she growled.

"I am Stephen, King of Regust and Zemire. I come for knowledge and for what aid may be found." Stephen stepped forward, hands held out to his sides. "I had not heard that petitioner's were met with drawn swords."

"These are dangerous times we have been brought to." she snapped. "One must protect oneself."

"And dangerous times that I plan to end. Take me to Amee." he ordered, gently.

"She is ill."

"I would not come were the need not great." he said. She looked uncertainly at him, biting her lower lip. "Please."

"Kaytlin, bring them." a voice commanded from inside. The girl sheathed her sword and, head bowed, motioned them to follow. She plucked a brand from the darkness and ignited it, then led the way to the sacred oracle chamber.

Amee sat there among the cushions, pale and frail amidst the vibrant colors. Stephen sat down across the flames from her. "Great Oracle, I need your help."

Amee raised her face to his and he gasped.

Her eyes were clouded marbles, oozing a green liquid from the corners.

"And I will try my best to give it, my king. The night I was robbed of my sight, I had one final vision. A castle on the other side of the Arundel Mountains, just beyond Silver Wood. This castle is black and from it spills great evil. There is a demon there. It has taken control of your brother, is using him as a host. You must save Catarine and find the other two who form the circle. Only the elemental circle can defeat him."

"And you think I am one of these elementals?" Stephen asked.

"Think back, Stephen. Was there never a time in your life that you did something remarkable? Something that no one else could do?" Amee prodded gently. Stephen searched his memory for a long time until it came to him:

He stood on the bank of the river, watching enviously as Mikel stood on the raft, fishing with Jalel. Their tutor was praising Mikel's casting when a large tree came sweeping down the swollen river. It shattered the raft, sending them both into the icy water. The current ripped Mikel away, dragging him under. He was going to drown! Stephen plunged his hands into the icy water...and it parted. A channel, dry as bleached bone, opened through the water, and Mikel lay on the ground coughing. Jalel snatched him up and ran back to the shore.

"I can control water. I've done it before. So, what does Catarine control? And where do I find the others?" he asked.

54

"They are along your path. You may even already know them. But as to their gifts, only they know for sure." Amee cocked her head toward Kaytlin. "You will rest here, tonight, and we will replenish your supplies. Tomorrow, you may go on. Your journey lies to the West."

Kathryn H. Sargeant   Blood Secrets: The Possession

Catarine screamed.

The girl turned around and reached for her. Drenched in blood, the girl smiled at the horror on Catarine's face.

"Why do you look at me so? Am I not your sister?"

"You are not Rose. Be gone, foul apparition!"

The girl shimmered, melted into another form. Christopher stood before her, holding out his hands, beseechingly. His pale hair was pink with clotted blood, his eyes empty holes; a sword protruded from his chest.

"Come with me, sister. Come to the Master. It will be so sweet. It is the only way," he purred. Catarine clapped her hands over her ears and squeezed her eyes shut. She took a deep breath and screamed the first thing that came to mind.

"By the power of the Elements, I defy thee! With the power of goodness and purity, I deny thee! Leave me, unclean one!"

Catarine sat up in bed, glaring at the night.

"You will not win, Mikel! You will not break me!" she vowed to the darkness.

There was a flash of blinding light. The landscape around her was devastation, littered with broken bodies and soaked with blood. The acrid smell of death and decay brought bile to her throat. Kaytlin stumbled, dragging the tip of her sword behind her in the dust. Was there no one left alive? Another flash up ahead, but weaker this time.

From the ashes, the demon rose up before her. They studied one another for a moment before it spoke, and its voice was the purr of a contented kitten, soft and low and appealing.

"Look around you, Kaytlin. This need not be the way it ends. Together, you and I could change it. We would keep the people safe. Come, rule at my side, surrender totally to me, to your blood. I will give you immortality. I will lay universes at your feet." Kaytlin shook her head. "Is it this form? My dear, I can take any form you find pleasing."

He shifted in rapid succession through many handsome forms, settling finally on the likeness of Stephen. He held out a hand to her and smiled.

"NO!" she shouted defiantly. The ground beneath her began to quake, ripping open, shoving upward in ragged spikes until she stood on a pinnacle of rock above a chasm of flames. The demon shook its four arms at her, claws clamped firmly on the bodies of her loved ones. Her mother, father, her uncle, and...Amee.

"Then die as they have!" he roared, throwing the bodies at the sliver she was standing on. It snapped, and she fell down, down, down.... into her own bed.

She rose and started gathering supplies.

Kathryn H. Sargeant   Blood Secrets: The Possession

Mikel stirred the pool at the foot of his obsidian throne. A picture began to ripple there, slowly coming to focus on a room. The walls were covered in rich silk tapestries, the carpets plush and colorful. The furniture was ornately carved. It was a young girl's dream.

Rose chipped at the mortar around the bars in the high window with her dinning fork. After a moment, she tried the bar. It wouldn't budge. She went back to pecking at the mortar. Mikel laughed. Rose spun, flattening herself against the wall, looking around.

"Hello, Rose. Enjoying your new comforts?"

"Mikel, you bastard! Where are you? Show yourself, you coward!" she shouted, anger making her voice squeak. Mikel appeared in front of her. Then, to either side of her. Suddenly, he was filling the entire room.

"Such hostility is so unbecoming, my lamb. Be sweet and I'll let you see your sister." he cajoled.

"Where is she? If you've harmed her, I swear I will…"

"You are in no position to make threats, my dear. Now, behave!" he snarled. With a small pop, all the Mikel figures winked out.

Palon helped Kaytlin drag the last of the supplies from the mountain and pile it near the horses.

"Can you manage?" she asked, wiping sweat from her brow. He nodded. "Good, then I will go rinse off some of this dirt." She disappeared inside the mountain but came back swiftly carrying a bundle under her arm and struck out for the lagoon. She dropped the bundle on the shore and quickly undressed before diving into the icy waters. She pulled herself along the bottom, reveling in the feeling of freedom. She felt free less and less these days, more like she was being controlled: she hated that. Swimming and hunting were the only things that assured her that her life was still her own. She danced among the coral and strands of algae until her burning lungs forced her back up through that painfully delicate layer between her freedom and those that sought to take it away. She broke through the surface in a shower of beads and tossed her wet mane from her face. She swam for a while and then ducked back under the water to pluck two pieces of coral. Kicking out, she traveled the bottom for a few minutes before surfacing. Jason sat on a stone by the water's edge, eyes fixed on the spot where she had gone under.

"What the hell do you think you're doing?" she demanded, hotly, crossing her arms over her chest. For once she was glad that the clear water darkened as it deepened. He turned his head to smile at her.

"Making sure you don't drown and indulging my taste for beauty. You are very beautiful, Kaytlin." he said, simply. She smiled and swam toward him, treading water at the base of the boulder.

"Give a beautiful girl a hand, then." she said, stretching her hand up to him. He rose and leaned down for her. She gripped his hand firmly, planting her feet on the rock, and pulled. He tumbled over the side and into the water. When he surfaced, she was already on the shore, wrapping her tunic tightly around herself. She laughed at him, sputtering and choking as he swam toward the shore. He stalked her along the sand, backing her against a tree, towering over her. He grabbed hold of her arm and she shuddered, convulsively.

"You. You are the nothing. You are the one that has been following me!"

"Have you seen Jason?" Stephen asked Palon. The young man grinned.

"He headed toward the lagoon. Kaytlin's there, too. Never seen a man so smitten or a girl so clueless." Palon laughed, cinching the rope tight. Stephen smiled wistfully.

"I'll give them some time, then. I want to speak to Amee once more before we go, anyway." Stephen turned back to the cave.

A long, agonized wail echoed through the corridors, followed by a deep rumbling chuckle.

"If you'd not resist, my dear, you'd not hurt." Mikel told her patiently. "You only have to say the words, Catarine."

"Burn in Hell!" she screamed at him. He shook his head, sadly.

"Wrong words." Lightning coursed through her body, bowing her back. Her teeth ground together, all her muscles clenching in pain. Her lungs constricted, her heart stopped for a split second. It was all the time he needed. His mind touched hers, searing her in excruciating communion. His mind pawed at hers, casually gleaning information through her pain. He spoke to her, mind to mind. "Join me, Catarine. Surrender your powers to me. It is your only hope."

"Never! I will die before I join you!" she shouted defiantly. In desperation, her mind lunged into his: Names, faces, scenes, deeds, and arcane knowledge surged through her mind, swirling and eddying like rushing water. It raced into the recesses of her brain, soothing her pains. Three names rose to the surface, lending her strength to push the demon, who she now knew as Krayboor, from her mind. She sealed herself behind an invisible shield and pondered the names curiously. She did not hear the anguished screams from Mikel, nor did she feel herself be carried back to her room.

Mikel shook with rage and pain. How did she know to do that? She had slipped through a chink he did not know he had, into his deepest plans and memories. This mere slip of a girl had managed to cause him great pain, and an emotion he had not felt in centuries: fear.

"Yes, I'm the one. I am bound to you somehow, Kaytlin. I could not let harm come to you or Amee. I am your wolf." Jason traced the curve of her cheek with his finger. "I will protect you with my life."

"I don't need your protection, I need your absence. Take your men and your prince and leave," she snarled, shoving him away. She turned and ran back to the cave. Palon shook his head as she rushed past. In her room, she dressed clumsily, her hands shaking. She would go hunting. Yes, that was what she would do. She would replenish the stores she had given to the soldiers. She strapped on quiver, wrist guards and dagger, and then pulled her green hunting cloak around her shoulders. Kaytlin hurried to Amee's chamber. "Amee, I'm going hunting. I will be back soon."

"Be careful, my dear." Amee's voice was tired as it answered from behind the curtain. Kaytlin reached for the curtain, but stopped just short of the silk. Her throat clenched painfully.

"I love you, Amee." she whispered.

"I love you, too, Kaytlin. Now, go or we won't have anything for supper." Kaytlin smiled and ran back down the corridor to the outside world.

Inside Amee's room, Amee lifted her fingers from Stephen's lips. She smiled at him, tired and worried and sad.

"I do love her. Loved her since the day her mother came to me and asked me to raise her. I swore to protect her with my hearts blood. Now, I am asking you to do the same."

"What would you have me do, Amee?" Stephen asked.

"Take her with you." Amee answered softly, her opaque eyes searching his face. "She is very special, Stephen, and very young. But, she may be useful to you, yet. Watch over her for me. Now, you must leave."

"I will." he vowed, kissing her hand. He rose to leave the chamber.

Kaytlin brushed past Jason and he grabbed her arm. She jerked it roughly from his grasp and glared at him. Her sizzling curse turned into a scream of horror. Over his shoulder, a monstrous black hand was slamming down from the clear blue sky. It smashed the mountaintop and continued down, crushing it like a child's model. Kaytlin ran for the mouth of the cave.

"Kaytlin, no!" Jason made a grab for her, catching a handful of cloak and tunic that ripped away in his hand like paper. She was gone. Heedless of the danger, he charged after her.

64

"Take good care of her my king. Farewell." Amee called after him, her voice thick with tears. Suddenly, there was a crashing roar from above. The ground pitched beneath his feet and the walls around him started to crumble. The passageway behind him filled with stone and dust. He ran. Up ahead, Jason swore, holding a struggling Kaytlin against his chest as he tried to drag her backward out of the cave. Without breaking stride, Stephen caught her flailing legs and together they raced down the corridor as it tried to swallow them, holding her tightly between them. They leapt out of the cave and into the blazing sun of midday.

"Run! The mountain is coming down! Run for the lagoon!" Palon shouted, pulling the horses into the trees. They ran, dust and boulders flying after them. Reaching the lagoon, they turned to watch the rising cloud of dust over the trees. There was nothing but silence. Even the waterfall was no more. They set Kaytlin down and she sank to her knees. Jason turned to Stephen, eyes filled with concern, hair wild.

"King Stephen, are you injured?" he asked. Stephen shook his head, his eyes locked on the girl rocking slowly back and forth on the ground beside him. A portion of her shoulder was uncovered: the star blazed on her shoulder like the summer sun off water. Kaytlin tipped her head back and howled.

Kathryn H. Sargeant   Blood Secrets: The Possession

Krayboor/Mikel sat back on the throne, laughing happily. Crushing that mountain and the bitch inside was the most fun he had had in days. If Kaytlin hadn't run back inside he could have gotten that meddling prince, too. But, no matter. His end would come. A stabbing pain behind his eyes made him groan. Damn the boy! He was fighting, again. Trying to win back his body, to force the evil out. Krayboor concentrated his will on wrapping Mikel tighter into the ball he had forced him into and shoved him to the very edge of his being. But, no matter how he tried, he could never force the boy completely out. Krayboor roared in rage, rocking the very walls of Nepanthier.

Catarine rolled over the information she had gleaned from the demon's mind. Poor Mikel. He was trying so hard to regain control. She was sorry she had ever doubted him. Now, she knew that Rose was here and well for the moment. She could turn her attention to the others.

She poured water into a glass and set it on the dressing table before her. She settled beside it and concentrated on Stephen's face. The water shimmered and then darkened. An oily swirl developed in the center, then spread out to form a picture. A picture of Stephen's sleeping face.

"Find Kaytlin and Jason. They are the keys. Find the stars that burn." she whispered. Stephen began to toss his head. "Find the stars that burn, they make up the circle."

The glass shattered.

Stephen sat up with a start and looked around the makeshift camp. Moonlight played off the still surface of the lagoon. Stephen jumped to his feet, kicking Jason as he rose. Jason was on his feet in an instant.

"Where is she?" Stephen demanded. "Where did she go?"

"I know. I'll get her back. Kraig, Matthew, Maden, come with me." Jason moved swiftly into the trees. The full moon lighted their way, stabbing through twisted branches. "Can you follow her trail, Kraig?"

"Yes."

"Good, you keep following her; I am going to circle around her." Jason melted into the darkness. The three tracked the girl in silence, watching for signs that they might be catching up to her. They turned a tree, and there she was, standing in a moonbeam, her face upturned. Tears sparkled on her cheek.

"Kaytlin?" Kraig called softly. She bolted like a deer into the foliage. "After her! Stephen wants her back!" They pounded after her, the need for stealth gone. Matthew swore.

"Had to call to her, didn't you?" he snarled, jumping a fallen tree.

"I didn't want to frighten her." Kraig gasped. "Shut up and run!" The trees thickened around them, becoming impenetrable in places. The thick trunks and branches seemed to echo ages past as they ran. "Where did she go?"

Kaytlin leapt a downed oak and kept running. She wanted away, to hide; there was nothing she could do against a force that could squash a mountain. She kept running, listening to the chase behind her. If she could just get there,

Kathryn H. Sargeant   Blood Secrets: The Possession

the power would protect her, hide her. She looked over her shoulder to gauge their distance...and slammed into something that went sprawling with her. Jason recovered first, pouncing on her and pinning her even as he jerked her arms behind her back. He tied them there with leather from his pouch.

"Easy, easy, Kaytlin. No one wants to hurt you." he assured her, pulling her to her feet.

"Let me go, I won't run, again." she coughed.

"No, let's take you where you were going, first. Then, we'll go back to camp." Jason declared, pulling her in the direction she'd been running. She dug in her heels.

"No. I wasn't going anywhere; I was just trying to get away. Let's go back to camp."

"I always lost you in this part of the forest. I want to see where you went. Now, let's go." he jerked her along in his wake.

"You are hurting my arm!" she cried in pain, and suddenly a wave of anger washed over her. She wanted to be free of him, to hurt him, to make him suffer. A streak of blue flame shot up Jason's arm. Startled, he let go and started slapping at the fire. Kaytlin dashed away from his flailing arms, but was brought crashing down by Kraig, who leapt after her. Kaytlin sobbed as he pulled her to her knees.

"Kaytlin, did I hurt you? Are you injured?" Kraig asked gently. A trickle of blood oozed from her nose and a blinding pain seared her eyes. When it passed, she was leaning against a tree, staring up into Jason's fiery eyes. Terror rooted itself in her heart. What was he going to do to her, now?

"How in the nine Hells," he began, his face a distorted mask of rage and pain, then shook himself. "No, it doesn't matter. Come along." He pulled her to her feet and along path. They had gone several yards when the trees suddenly opened up into a large glade. Their jaws dropped open.

The obelisk glowed brightly in the moonlight, standing roughly six feet tall it pulsed with power. The white marble was carved with symbols and letters diligently crafted by a loving hand. Kaytlin looked at it miserably and tensed at their gasps of astonishment. Kraig went to one knee before it, bowing his head reverently.

"What is it?" Jason whispered, his voice filled with awe.

"It's a shrine." Kraig said.

"Why here?" Matthew asked.

"Because this is where my mother is buried." Kaytlin sighed. "Untie me, Jason."

"No," he said coldly.

"I have to get something from the shrine."

"Tell me what it is and I will get it." Jason replied.

"You cannot. You will defile the shrine. Only a priestess can attend a shrine of Shondea." Kraig snapped.

"Please, Kraig, don't let him defile my shrine!" she sobbed.

Keys fumbled in the lock. Rose sprang from the chair beside the door, and lifted the water pitcher high over her head, holding her breath. The door swung open. A small creature entered bearing a tray. From behind, it looked like a sweet potato that had started to rot, from its' stubby little limbs to its' black shock of wiry hair. Rose brought the pitcher crashing down on top of its' pointed head. It fell facedown amid the clatter of broken pottery and the crash of crystal dishes. Rose used her foot to roll the thing away from the door. Checking to make sure the hall was clear, she slipped outside and closed the door softly behind her. She sped off down the corridor to the left, keeping to the shadows. The décor was less than to be desired. Tapestries depicting torture scenes hung from the walls, and statues of horrendous demons and other misshapen creatures littered the alcoves. Running feet. She slipped behind a group of statues and crouched down. A platoon of demons marched by, oblivious to her. She leaned against the marble and then grunted in revulsion. The group was a ring of small ogres, each trying to mount the same human girl. The horror on her face was heartbreaking. Rose hurried away from the terrifying scene. She tiptoed through the corridor, occasionally peeking through spy holes in the doors. If she could find Catarine, that would be wonderful, but if she managed to find a way out, that would be even better. She crossed a stairwell and started down the twisting steps. She counted a hundred before she reached the landing below.

Kathryn H. Sargeant   Blood Secrets: The Possession

She eased into the dim light of guttering torches and crept along, feeling her way on the slick stone. Footsteps echoed on the steps: lots of them, and in a rush. Rose dove into the first room she came across and pulled the door shut. A squad of demons marched by, growling and snarling at each other. She couldn't go back into the passageways unarmed. Rose looked around. A scream of fury bubbled past her lips.

She was back in the same room she had started in. The door locked with a soft snick.

Catarine stood at her window, fists clenched in determination. She would make it work this time. She took a deep breath, calming the shaking of her limbs, and closed her eyes. She drew on the store of knowledge that she had so painfully acquired, allowing the information she needed to gather at the front of her mind. She let loose the fluttering in her soul and opened her senses to the night. Deep inside her, a wind began to blow softly, then to grow, a wordless tune that swelled like a tempest. She opened her mouth and the tempest drained from her, rushing around the room, wrenching open the shutters. It swirled around her, gathering in the center of the room, taking on a human form. It bowed slightly to her.

"What would you have of me, child?" it asked in a soft whistling tune.

Kathryn H. Sargeant   Blood Secrets: The Possession

"I summoned you to see if I could. So that I would be sure of my escape when the time came." she stuttered.

"When your time comes, child, call Lyrissa. I will come to your aid." the wind creature assured her.

"Wait! There is something you can do. I tried to send a message to Stephen, but I am not sure that he got it. Can you tell him we are safe for the moment and that he needs to find Kaytlin and Jason?" she said.

"He has found them already, my lady. But, the mountain was destroyed, and I do not know if Stephen and Kaytlin survived. I will go learn what I may and then I will return. Fare thee well." the wind rushed out the window. Catarine pulled the shutters closed, then staggered to the bed, weak with exhaustion.

"I promise you, he will not." Kraig vowed. He stepped between Jason and the shrine, dagger in hand. Jason stared at him incredulously and then looked from Kraig to Kaytlin. She turned her back on Kraig and he sliced through her bonds. "Go get what you need."

A loud crack splintered the night, exploding trees and tearing the earth up in clumps. A bolt of blue steel shot from the very moon itself and shattered the marble like glass. All was still. A silvery-white light surrounded the broken remains, gathered in its' center and coalesced into a human form. The lady stood tall and regal in her flowing spirit gown, her long chestnut hair blowing in an unreal wind. Her oval, cobalt blue eyes gazed lovingly at Kaytlin and her delicate lips pulled back in a warm smile. She held her hands out to her daughter, beckoning.

"Mother?" Kaytlin whispered, throatily. She drifted to stand before the apparition. Natahlia reached out and caressed her young daughter's cheek, gently touching her hair. She stared a long time, as if memorizing each feature. A tear slid down her cheek.

"Listen well, Kaytlin. I am only allowed to speak of your future in riddle form. Four to hands, in circle round, be rain and flame and wind and ground. Unlock the lockless; know the unknowing, blind with traitors blood the shadow unknowing. The she beasts will fight with lion's rage. Go now, child, and set the stage." Natahlia smiled reassuringly at her. "Trust your blood, trust yourself." She began to fade.

74

"No, Mother! Don't leave me alone!" Kaytlin cried, reaching desperately toward Natahlia.

"Dear one, you are not now, nor will you ever be, alone." Natahlia's voice purred as she disappeared completely. Kaytlin squared her shoulders and knelt. From the ruins she pulled a silver shield, a short dagger, a bow of supple white wood, and a quiver filled with arrows. Lastly, she pulled a long sword in a silver and green scabbard from the rubble.

"Kraig, will you help me carry these to camp?" she asked her voice barely audible. He moved swiftly to her side and she loaded his arms. She rose and took up the quiver and bow. With mumbled thanks, she turned and started back to camp.

Stephen was waiting anxiously for them. He paced by the fire, muttering under his breath. Kaytlin walked past him as if he were not there to a packhorse where she began tucking away her weapons. He looked questioningly at Jason. Jason shrugged. The sun peeked over the horizon and the camp began to stir. Quickly, they were packed and ready to ride. Kaytlin took one last look at the remains of her home and then moved to where Kraig sat on his horse.

"May I ask one more favor of you, Kraig?" she asked. He nodded, gravely. "May I ride with you on this journey?" In answer, he simply put his hand down for hers. She swung up behind his saddle and settled herself for the long ride.

"Which way?" Palon asked.

"East. To the Plains of Corwith." Kaytlin responded. Jason glared at Kraig, then turned and spurred his horse eastward.

Catarine stared out the window at the mountains beyond. A storm was brewing atop the jagged crags, lightning dancing in its purple hair. A wind whipped her hair across her eyes as it howled through the room, lifting her silken tresses in a golden banner to be snatched and twisted around. Her hazel eyes glittered and heat shimmered off her skin as she fed the growing tempest. Suddenly, the wind tore away from her, chaos and destruction its' only desire. Her head dropped back and her breathing became ragged gasps as she fought to regain control, but it was too strong for her. She collapsed onto the floor in exhaustion and the wind escaped out the window. Next time, she would have to remember not to make it so strong so fast.

Torq entered the room, looking down curiously at the human on the floor. He had been assured she was desirable among her kind, but he just didn't see it. He scooped her up and put her on the bed, jerking the covers roughly over her. He glanced at the window and the shutters slammed closed on the storm outside.

"Keep up your efforts, girl. The master will have use for them soon enough. He will greatly enjoy using your storm against your betrothed."

Kaytlin watched the green plain, intently, counting on her fingers while the rest waited.

"Now!" she cried and Kraig let his arrow fly across the plain. It was snatched from the air and flung yards off the mark. Kraig notched another arrow. "Now!" This time the arrow flew true, embedding itself in a small rise of earth. Kaytlin turned to the assembled men.

"The Breath of Corwith comes every five beats. Be braced for it or it will carry you off. Or worse, knock you down. We leave the horses here. They'll never make it across the plain and we must get across before nightfall. There is no piece of ground big enough for us to camp on there." she explained.

"What are the dangers?" Stephen asked. She looked at him as though he were thick.

"You don't know about the Plains of Corwith? No man fears beauty. Corwith knew this. So, he created beautiful deaths. Do not go near the flowers. Watch." she counted to six, then threw a stick at a black tulip far away to the right. A cloud of black tinged green rose from it, hovered a moment, then drifted away.

"Poison." Kraig said, simply. He pointed at a peach striped rose. "What about that one?" She picked up another stick, counted to six, and threw. The stick brushed the very edge of a leaf on the plant, and it erupted in a ball of fire.

It burned out quickly, leaving a large area of ground around it destroyed. She pointed to a ring of daisies.

"Step inside that ring, and you will sink under the ground. There is only one thing on this plain that is not deadly and that is this." She plucked a blue flower from the edge of the field and held it up. It resembled an exploding star, the white veining adding the illusion of movement. "Cellestrar. Don't breathe too deeply of it, it intoxicates. The roots can be chewed to ease pain. It has a dark side, too, but not a deadly one. Please, be careful where you step. And try to remember to count. If you're braced at every fifth beat, you will be safe."

Kaytlin turned and stepped onto the emerald green of the plain. Two more careful steps and the wind slammed into her like a fist. It lasted only seconds and then all was still. She took eight more steps and the wind slammed into her, again. Jason walked to her left, a couple of steps behind. On the next lull, he came abreast of her, matching his pace to hers.

"I know what you are doing with Kraig. Don't use him to play me a fool." he snapped. She stopped, staring at him in astonishment.

"I don't need him to play you a fool, Jason. You do that well enough on your own!" she snarled, then spun on her heel and stalked away. She had gone several steps when she realized that she had forgotten to count.

Kathryn H. Sargeant   Blood Secrets: The Possession

Rose lay upon the cold stone of the floor, feeling the storm rumble through the castle. Her sobs of frustration and self-loathing rang sharply in her ears and she slammed her fists repeatedly against the stone. She kept replaying the scene in her chambers over and over in her mind, picking out the errors she had made. Lorell would be so disappointed. Lorell. Was her friend even still alive? The thought burned her more than the humiliation of her failure. She drug herself to her feet and looked around the room.

The four-poster canopy bed sat against the far wall, the curtains pushed aside and hanging lamely. The rose and lavender bedclothes lay crumpled on the floor and the marble vanity leered at her from its place near the armoire. The desk sat morosely by the window, its rounded corners mocking her. There was no sharp angle or object to be seen anywhere in the room. She supposed she could take the big ugly iron washbasin and smash herself in the skull with it. Then, at least, Catarine would have one less person to worry about.

The iron washbasin.

Rose ran to the stand and picked up the heavy bowl. It just might work. She took it to the ornate fireplace and set it down, then drug over the marble nightstand. She thrust the nightstand over the flames and set the bowl on top of it. She wrapped her hand tightly in a piece of linen and punched the vanity mirror until it shattered. Now, if she could just build a mold....

The Breath of Corwith slammed against Kaytlin's unguarded body and sent her pitching forward. Her arms wheeled as she toppled headlong toward a cluster of peach striped roses. Strong hands seized her, pulling her back against a firm chest and held her there. Kraig panted heavily as they stood against another blast of wind, then he slowly released her.

"That was too close." he gasped.

"You were so far behind..."Kaytlin said, her voice ripe with surprise. "Kraig, you risked running to save me?"

"I, I didn't think about it." Kraig mumbled, flushing under her stare. She rose on her tiptoes and kissed his cheek.

"Again, you are my champion. What did I do for the Great Mother to grant me you?" she asked, smiling up at him.

"Kaytlin, are you hurt?" Stephen demanded, stopping beside them as another blast smashed into them. Kaytlin shook her head. "Be more careful, Kaytlin."

She nodded then moved off. It was slow going. They were halfway across when someone shouted in alarm. Stephen whirled in time to see Jason sliding beneath the soil of a fairy ring. Kraig, only a few steps ahead, turned and began uncoiling a rope from around his waist. He tossed the end to Stephen and then, without a word, dove into the sucking soil and disappeared. Men hurried to help Stephen hold the swiftly disappearing rope. It snapped tight, jerking them forward.

Kathryn H. Sargeant   Blood Secrets: The Possession

"HAUL!" Stephen cried. Slowly, grudgingly the ground gave the rope back. Just when they were about to give up hope, a hand shot from the soil. Kaytlin grabbed it and pulled with all her might. With a tremendous pop, the two men popped out of the ground like potatoes. They lay gasping on the ground, coughing dirt from their lungs. Kaytlin used her water skin to rinse their faces.

"Brother, you are insane." Jason gasped at Kraig. "And I am in your debt. Thank you."

"It was nothing you wouldn't have done for me." Kraig shrugged.

"How many times do I have to say it?" Stephen demanded, angrily. "BE CAREFUL!!!" He helped them to stand, and then got them moving, again. He put his hand on Kaytlin's arm to hold her back. "Little sister, I need to talk to you."

"What is it?" she asked, pleased that he had called her by that endearment. She was beginning to care for him, to look to him like an older brother.

"Be careful of this game you are playing, girl. I have come to care for you very deeply, but I will not let you bring those two men to destruction. I have precious little resources enough to have two men waste each other over a mere girl. Do you understand?" Kaytlin stared at him as the Breath lifted her hair like a banner, snapping it into her eyes. When it dropped, her eyes were shiny with tears

"I understand, your highness. I understand that all you men think you are gods on earth, and no poor helpless female can resist you. I understand that you

Kathryn H. Sargeant   Blood Secrets: The Possession

think all women are merely schemers and troublemakers." she ripped her arm from his grasp. "I understand you are all thick headed and despicable. Now, you understand this: I am not playing any games. But I do promise you that when this is over I am leaving and may all the gods and goddesses damn my eternal soul if I ever lay eyes on you or your dim-witted little lackey friend Jason again!" She waited for the next Breath to pass, then spun and stalked off, tears pouring down her cheeks. She rushed past Kraig and Maden, who shot Stephen a questioning look. Kraig hurried after her.

"Kaytlin, what is wrong?" Kraig demanded, coming up beside her.

"Nothing you can help with, friend. Let's just get across this thrice-damned plain and be done with this whole asinine venture," she sobbed. Kraig tried to lay a comforting hand on her arm, but she hurried away. He turned his angry grey eyes to Stephen.

Kaytlin rested against the trunk of a great oak, watching as the last of the men stepped off the plain. Jason sat across the way, talking softly with Stephen, who kept shooting her worried glances. She ignored them, her gaze fixed on the plain. Something was not right about the area they had just passed through. Something strange... A shadow fell over her and she looked up. Stephen looked down at her, his face awash with shame and concern.

"I owe you an apology. I forgot that you were not a court maiden, used to bending men with your charms, making them fight over you for your amusement. Please, forgive me. I still see you as a little sister." he smiled.

"I had begun to feel like you were a brother." she shrugged, her eyes drifting back to the plain. "We both said things we didn't mean. Let's forget it happened."

"What is troubling you?"

"Something about where we passed. It isn't right. I just can't place it." Kaytlin pushed herself to her feet and unbuckled the sword from her waist. She handed it to Stephen. "Take this: I have a feeling it was meant for you." She unslung the shield from her back and walked purposefully to where Kraig sat leaning against a tree, his head back and his eyes closed. She cleared her throat and he smiled up at her.

"Just resting." he said. She knelt beside him, holding out the shield.

"I want you to have this."

"I can't take that, it's a gift from your mother." he frowned.

"You are the only one who recognized or respected my shrine. You have protected me from the beginning and you are very dear to me. I want to give you this because we don't know what we are going into and you may need it. Please, Kraig, please take it. I need to keep my friends close and safe," she pleaded, touching his cheek. He cupped her hand against the side of his face.

"Then, I would be honored to accept your shield. On one condition."

"Which is?"

"You name me your champion." he leaned close to her. "All the blue flowers, the Cellestrar, have been plucked from the path we took across the Plain. There is something dark in our midst. Please." Kaytlin nodded, pulling a small chain from around her neck. Dangling from it was a simple emerald shaped like a crescent moon. Kaytlin took a deep breath and pitched her voice so that it would be heard.

"Kraig, my friend, will you become my champion and protector?"

"I swear to protect you from all foes, even if it means my life." he vowed, taking the necklace and slipping it over his head. Kaytlin stood up and turned to look for Jason. He was sitting hunched on a rock at the edge of the plain, staring dejectedly at the ground. She walked over and laid a hand on his arm.

"Be alert, Jason. We have a traitor in our midst."

The molten liquid oozed its way down along the gold frame, cooling slightly as it flowed. It eased into corners and along edges, tempering itself against the wooden backing. Sweat dripped into Rose's eyes. She held the washbasin by its edges, careful not to splash the molten glass. She had bent the mirror frame into a crude form and she prayed silently to Shondea that it would serve. The heat from the iron burned through the bedspread she was using as a shield and she groaned softly. Almost done. She set the basin aside, twitching the spread away and smiled at the holes burned in the linen. Her hands, shaking from heat and exhaustion, were only mildly red. Rose used a corner of the ruined spread to wipe her face. She waited for the glass to start solidifying and began to scrape the edges back. Not too thin, she didn't want it to break. Just be sharp. Slowly, her little makeshift dagger took form

Lorell would be proud. The thought brought her comfort.

Shadows flitted through the camp. Sparks shot occasionally from the coals as the fires burned down, lending the silver bark on the trees around them an eerie flickering life. Maden crouched low to the ground beside his packs, carefully tucking the blue flowers out of sight. Matthew leaned against a tree, disinterestedly surveying the camp. It was a slow watch.

How easy it would be to slice their throats while they slept. Like lambs to the slaughter, they slept deep and peacefully. And that sanctimonious bastard over there, with his arms wrapped around her shoulders. How sweet it would be to bash his ribs in, still his bleeding heart. How sensitive to recognize the shrine,

Kathryn H. Sargeant   Blood Secrets: The Possession

how touching to come to her defense time and again. How utterly sickening it was to watch her offer herself to him. No matter. It would all come to naught. They would all come to naught. Maden joined him by the tree. He could feel the rage radiating from his brother like heat. He followed Matthew's gaze to the couple lying at the edge of the camp, away from the others. Kaytlin nestled in Kraig's protective arms, her head lying against his bicep, his cheek resting atop her head. There was something sweet and innocent in the embrace. He felt his stomach twist.

"I stored them safely away." Maden whispered.

"Good. I dare say they will come in handy. Look at them. Why didn't Jason slice him down when he had the chance?" Matthew growled.

"Perhaps, he is waiting for a time when it can look like an accident. Perhaps he is a coward." Maden shrugged. "Anyway, it doesn't matter. Soon, our Lord will take possession of all the land and its' occupants. If you serve him faithfully, perhaps he will grant you the young seeress."

"Perhaps."

Lorell stood on the courtyard wall, surveying the activity. The clearing and rebuilding was going much better than she had hoped. Already, the people had managed to remove most of the rubble of Ariangard and had rebuilt several houses from the salvageable materials. The city was coming alive, once more. Her people would not be squashed so easily.

"Lorell?" She turned to see a young man walking toward her. He stopped and gave a short bow. "Good news. I have two falcons whose wings have healed. We can send the messages you wanted to Silver Wood and Regust."

"Excellent. Stephen will have an army. We'll see to that."

They traveled slowly through clinging underbrush and tearing branches. The silence was deafening. Kaytlin walked beside Stephen.

"There is something wrong here," she said.

"I know. Where are all the birds, the animals, the insects?" he asked. "It's been almost a week and we've heard not a sound." He was silent for a long minute. "I promised Amee that I would take care of you, you know?"

"A foolish promise. I have someone to take care of me. Someone who does not condemn me for things that I have not done." she said simply.

"Will you never forgive me for that?"

"I forgave you. But I do not forget. Ever. I am told my mother was the same way."

"Your mother was sister to Gregory?"

"Yes. He refused to let her marry my father, who was a minstrel. Gregory threatened to have my father killed if he did not leave the kingdom. No sister of his would waste herself on a penniless minstrel. So, they fled to a secret cove by the Thundering Seas and married there. Gregory hunted them down and drug my mother back to the Blackthorn. I was born seven months later." Kaytlin stared into space. "My father was killed. When mother found out, she was terrified. She thought I would be his next target. Hard to marry off a princess who has a child by a commoner, you know. So, during a horrible snowstorm she wrapped me in furs and fled into the night. She never forgot her brother's betrayal. It was fresh in her mind at all times. I am much like my mother. No slight is ever forgotten."

"Why Kraig?" he asked softly.

"Because, he recognized my shrine for what it was and refused to let anyone defile it. He respects my religion and me. And he has never tried to harm or control me. He understands that that is something no man can or should do." she glanced sidelong at him. "And he asked me to. Had it not been for the little scene on the plain, it would have been you I sought protection from. That's what you are really asking, is it not?"

"Yes. I suppose it is."

Maden strode up to them.

Kathryn H. Sargeant   Blood Secrets: The Possession

"There is a glade up ahead; it might be a good place to camp for the night."

"We could use some rest, Stephen. Let's go ahead and stop for the day." Kaytlin sighed. Stephen looked around. Everyone looked exhausted.

"Come, troops. We'll make camp up ahead and try to get some rest."

Kaytlin surveyed the clearing. It was large and dry with a lush canopy of intertwined branches overhead. The trees here were old and strong and tall. In the center of the clearing was a ring of three large boulders. The ground was soft with moss and slightly spongy under her feet. She sank to the ground and stretched out and was soon fast asleep. Somewhere overhead, a falcon screamed.

Matthew walked through the underbrush, a pack hoisted across his shoulders. His eyes searched the trees while his ears strained for any sound: he had to hurry, he might be missed soon. He rounded a fallen knot of twisted trees and slammed into a huge black stump.

Torq turned to look down at him with mild contempt.

"You humans certainly have a problem with balance." Torq growled. Matthew pulled himself up off the ground.

"Only when we bounce off lurking walls." he snapped. Torq grinned at him, jagged teeth glistening.

"Excuses are the food of the incompetent. Have you brought them?"

"Of course. There are at least a hundred here." Matthew thrust the pack at Torq.

"The master has another job for you. You must get her up on one of those rocks."

"How am I supposed to do that?"

"Think of something, human. Think of something." Torq smirked. Matthew blinked. Only the giant's smile remained.

"Master, I have the Cellestrar and I gave Matthew your orders. What is your next command?" Torq asked, bowing before the obsidian throne. Krayboor rubbed his hands together, eagerly.

"Start the distilling process and make the room ready in the east tower. Everything a young girl could want. We will have another guest, soon. Has the third column reported in?"

"No, master. Last we heard, they were pursuing the remnants of the amazons through the forest."

"Excellent. You have your orders, Torq. Get busy." Torq bowed and left the room. Krayboor leaned forward to gaze into the pool at the foot of the throne. A picture swirled there of Kaytlin's sleeping face. "Soon, my dear. Soon."

"I think we can do it."

"Kaytlin, wake up." Stephen shook her shoulder. She rubbed her face, blearily and yawned.

"Is it time to head out, already?" she asked. Stephen smiled at her.

"No. We want to try to contact Catarine. Jason has an idea."

"We should try to get up a little higher. I think if we get up on those rocks and link hands, we could try to open a channel." Jason told her excitedly. She blinked at him, groggily, then nodded.

91

"Sounds like a good idea to me. Let's try it." Stephen pulled her to her feet and gave her a gentle push toward the nearest boulder. "What gave you the idea, Jason?"

"Actually, Matthew suggested the rocks, said it might add the element of air to the mix." Jason explained. Kaytlin scampered up the middle moss-slick rock and surveyed her surroundings. Stephen pulled himself up on her left and reached for her hand.

A sudden wave of dizziness washed over her and the heat seemed to increase a hundredfold. Her very blood seemed to boil beneath her skin and she gasped.

"The dream!"

The sky bellowed like an angry beast above them and the canopy of branches suddenly wrenched apart. Jason slipped to the ground as a maelstrom erupted around them. Foul smelling winds ripped at them and she could hear yelling. Yet, she knew that if she could just reach Jason's hand....

"JASON!" she screamed, reaching frantically for him, but his horror filled eyes stared past her. The crushing pressure on her left hand made her turn to Stephen. She screamed. A monstrous ebony hand tore through the treetops, swooping down toward the figures on the rocks, its' fingers spread wide.

Maden threw himself at Stephen, tearing him down from the boulder and pulling Kaytlin off balance. She swayed precariously in the wind, her eyes riveted on the hand that reached for her. Kraig roared, leaping to slash at the abomination as the fingers closed tightly around her, plucking her into the stormy sky. She struggled against the iron fingers, turning her head to see the ground disappear.

"NO!" she heard Stephen scream.

Matthew slammed Jason to the ground, driving his knee hard into Jason's stomach. He sneered in Jason's face as the winds buffeted them.

"You don't stand a chance against the master, boy. You can't even save your pitiful self from me, what makes you think you can save the girls from him?" Matthew glanced up to see Maden kicking a stunned Stephen and Kraig swinging his sword madly at the departing hand. He drew his dagger and raised it above his head. "Now, you die!"

An arrow embedded itself in Matthew's wrist, piercing straight through, and he dropped the dagger. A screeching filled the air around him as he staggered toward his brother, clutching his wrist close. A shaft of black smoke coalesced between them and they raced to jump inside. It swallowed them. The wind tore the trees from the ground, tossing them around like twigs. A massive oak hurtled toward an unconscious Stephen. Kraig pulled the shield from his back and dove....

Rose lay flat on the four-poster bed, thinking. Somehow, she had to get him in here with her and she could end this. The heat in the room was cloying. She moved to the window and opened the shutters to the raging storm outside. There always seemed to be a storm outside. Unlacing her gown, she breathed deeply of the cool wet rain and let her dress slip to the floor, unnoticed. The fat droplets cooled her skin, steaming in the heat of her body. Drenched, she stood shivering in the shower of cold water pouring through the window. Maybe, it wouldn't work after all.

The door behind her opened, and Mikel walked in. He snatched the bedspread from the floor and strode across the room to wrap around her shoulders. She sank into him, and he carried her back to her bed, laying her down in the twisted sheets.

"Rose, Rose, darling Rose. What are you thinking? Pneumonia is not a pretty way to die." he chided. Her hands twisted in the sheets as he leaned closer.: He brushed his lips across her burning forehead. Her arm drifted up: the glass dagger glinted in a sudden flash of lightning as she drove it with all her strength down into his neck. His hands shot to his throat as blood spurted from the wound. Mikel staggered backward, and Rose watched in fascinated horror as the bleeding began to slow, then stopped. The glass slid from his flesh with a sickening sucking sound, and the hole sealed itself, leaving only a small white slit to mark its' passing. Mikel's eyes blazed crimson, the pupils narrow slits of black flame. Then, he laughed. The glass dagger turned to powder in his palm and he let it trickle through his fingers.

"How clever. I see you will be the one who keeps me on my toes." he rasped. He reached out a long finger to touch her between the eyes. Rose's spine twisted in agony as a thousand bees stung her at once. She glared at him through swimming eyes.

"I will kill you. Make no mistake about that." she swore. He laughed.

"I look forward to your next attempt. Tell me, would you like to see something? Or should I say, someone? I think you'll be very interested." he assured her, passing his hand between their faces. A black cloud formed between them, swirling and twisting until it was as opaque as a mirror. It warped and shimmered, and a picture formed along its' surface: A young girl, lying deathly still, her chestnut hair spread on the pillow behind her. In sudden fury, she exploded against the chains holding her down, roaring in frustration as she wrenched the iron manacles to and fro. Then, she was still, again, catching her breath. The manacles began to glow with a soft blue light. Flames erupted along the links of the chain, flames that quickly died. The girl began to sniffle and Rose could see a tiny trickle of blood seep from the side of her nose. Her head snapped around, her eyes widening as Torq entered the room. He stared down at the helpless girl and then reached for her hair. Mikel passed a hand through the cloud, scattering it.

"Kaytlin." he said, simply. "She has her mother's fire and her father's heart. It will come in handy quite nicely." He strode from the room, locking the door behind him.

"You will dress, or I will dress you, little sister."

That's what the giant had said to her and from the look in his eyes she had known he meant it. Kaytlin laced the bodice of the white gown loosely, her back to him. He stood against the wall, looking at the nails on his fingers, humming softly, but she knew he was watching her. She sat down on the edge of the bed and slid her feet into the satin slippers he had laid there after fetching water for her to clean herself.

"There are combs there, also." he said. She ran one through her tangled hair and then dropped it on the bed. He shrugged. "Are you prepared?" She nodded. Torq pushed away from the wall and opened the door. He led her down one corridor after another and up and down several crumbling staircases until they came to a brightly lit passageway that ended in a large set of ebony double doors. Torq knocked three times and the doors swung open. Kaytlin marched through them and into a private dining room. Torq pulled back one of the velvet chairs and she sat down. The sudden snick of manacles locking made her jump. Her wrists and ankles were now secured to the chair.

Kathryn H. Sargeant   Blood Secrets: The Possession

"You may go, Torq."

Kaytlin turned her head. Mikel stood at the other end of the table, his back to them as he watched the flames in the hearth, a steaming goblet in his hand. He turned and smiled at Kaytlin. "That gown is so much more becoming than your filthy tunic and ripped breeches." He walked down the table to perch on its edge before her, carefully setting the goblet aside, and reached out a finger to trace her cheek. Growling, she jerked her head back.

"Why, Kaytlin, whatever is the matter?" he asked, using Amee's voice. Her eyes widened, filling with tears, and then she roared with rage. She tried to lunge at him but her bonds kept her pinned to the chair. He chuckled. "Calmly, little lovely. Your face is red as blood."

"How dare you mock her memory? Murderer! You killed my mother, my Amee, my uncle! Don't you dare touch me, again." she snapped at his outstretched hand like a wounded wolf. He took hold of a lock of her hair and tugged playfully.

"You belong to me, Kaytlin, and I will touch you anytime that I wish. Indeed, there will come a time when you beg for my touch." Mikel pulled her head back so he could look down into her eyes. "Join me, Kaytlin. I can give you pleasures, riches beyond your wildest fantasies. Be mine, rule at my side and I will lay worlds at your feet. I'll give you the stars for jacks and the moon for a ball." He leaned down until his lips brushed her ear. "Surrender yourself to me, join with me, and we will conquer the very universe." In a flash, Kaytlin jerked her head to the side and sank her teeth into the flesh of his cheek. He howled in pain as they sliced through the skin and blood spurted everywhere. His fingers

dug into her mouth, forcing her jaws apart and he staggered away from her, his

hand pressed against his face.

"Was that a firm enough no for you or do I need to be less subtle?" she

asked. Mikel laughed, pulling his hand away from the pale circular scar on his

face.

"My little hell cats will leave me many mementoes." he fingered his throat.

"And I will cherish them all. But, now, I will make you a promise: You will join

me. You see, I had a little nepenthe brewed especially for you, my dear. I think

you will find that the Cellestrar will help change your attitude in many ways." He

lifted the goblet to her lips. "Now, be a good little girl and drink it down." Kaytlin

clamped her lips closed and began tossing her head from side to side. Her hair

lashed at him, stung her own eyes as she tossed it madly. Mikel seized a

handful of her mane and jerked her head around to face him.

"I will be victorious!" he snarled, viciously prying her lips open with the rim

of the goblet. He poured its steaming contents into her mouth and held it closed.

The sickeningly sweet liquid burned as it raced down her throat and she gagged

convulsively. The nepenthe scorched through her veins like a black storm and

as her memory faded into oblivion her eyes widened in a hollow stare. Kaytlin

blinked vacantly up at Mikel as he wiped the potion from her chin.

"Who am I?" she stammered. "Who are you?"

"You are my consort, Kaytlin. You belong to me and you will obey me in

all things." He walked around the chair, eyeing her critically. "I prefer my ladies

Kathryn H. Sargeant   Blood Secrets: The Possession

with longer hair." He chanted a verse and Kaytlin's hair began to grow, coiling over her shoulders like a chestnut rope.

"Kaytlin....Kaytlin!" Jason bolted upright in the dim light.

"Lay back, warrior. You are not yet rested." A young woman eased him back down onto the pallet and recovered his partially naked form. She gently wiped his fevered brow with a cool cloth.

"Kaytlin." he choked in a hoarse whisper. She shook her head, sadly.

"If you speak of the girl with the chestnut hair, we could not reach her in time. She is gone."

"Who are you?" he asked, warily.

"I am Nicora, sister to Mishala, Queen of the Amazons. We received your falcon, and came to your aid." She fumbled with an oil lamp and the tent brightened.

"We sent no falcon."

"Forgive me. I misspoke. Lorell, the king's ambassador, sent for us. She explained the king's quest and that he had only twenty men. We came to offer the remnants of our army to him." She sat back on her heels, unbuckling her green and gold breastplate. She tossed it casually aside and shook out her long white hair. Her deep blue eyes glowed warm and sympathetic as they touched his.

"Where is Stephen? And what happened?"

"We were traveling toward the Plain to meet you when we heard the commotion. We attacked. The hand was already in the air with the girl. There was chaos, men running, trees flying." She shook her head, again. "When it was over, we found only three survivors."

"Did one of them have a shield?"

"Yes. Truly, it was the shield that kept them both from being smashed by a tree. It grew to protect them. It must be very powerful magic." Nicora handed him his tunic. Jason nodded. The tent flap moved and Stephen and Kraig ducked inside.

"I told you he only needed a nap to be good as new." Kraig said, giving Stephen a good-natured slap on the back.

"Welcome back to the land of the living." Stephen said. "Up for a march?"

Natahlia stood beside the four-poster bed, its rich satin draperies pulled aside. Among the silken down comforters and plush pillows, Kaytlin lay on her back, eyes closed in blissful sleep. Natahlia glanced around the room and sighed. It was filled with warm fur rugs and silken pillows. Lavish gowns hung in the armoire and gilt slippers were stacked in neat rows across its' bottom. Gold thread throws adorned the fainting couch and the tapestries along the walls were all of picnics and hunts. Truly, a dream. These were things that Kaytlin had never had in her austere life and could only dream of having. But, the price was a harsh one. Natahlia pushed the hair out of the young girl's closed eyes.

"You are no demon's slave, child. You are Kaytlin, my dear daughter, Kaytlin the brave and strong-willed. Wake up and remember. Remember that yours is a quest to destroy this demon." Kaytlin's head began to move slowly from side to side underneath her mother's hand. A low moan issued from her lips and her body began to writhe in pain, her eyes snapped open, focusing on Natahlia, and her hands flew to her temples.

"Ohhhh." she groaned. "Oh, mother, it hurts! Please, mother, please make the pain stop." Natahlia took her daughter's head between her hands and gently massaged her temples and eyes, and the pain began to ease.

"You are a young, innocent child who still has much to learn. Catarine has knowledge you need." she whispered as she stroked Kaytlin's head. "I know you are scared, but trust yourself. Not all the right paths are clearly marked. Remember, trust your intuition." A key rattled in the door and Natahlia vanished. The door swung open and Matthew and Torq strode in. For a moment, she thought Matthew had been captured, too, but then his eyes roamed over her and he leered.

"The Master does have good taste." he said, his eyes lingering on her uncovered thigh. Kaytlin sat up, pulling her legs underneath her. She wanted to tear out his throat with her teeth, but she widened her eyes, darting her glance from one to the other, and breathed in harsh little gasps.

"Don't you remember me, Kaytlin?" Matthew asked, pleasantly. She bit her lip and shook her head. "We used to be very intimate friends, before the Master claimed you. I am Matthew, the Master's Captain of the Guard. We have

102

come to take you to see your sister-consort, Catarine. She is very upset and we thought you might calm her down. Come." He held out his hand to her. She noticed the giant looking at her, thoughtfully, as she slid from the bed. Timidly, she placed her hand in Matthew's and let him lead her from the room. The giant followed in silence as they walked the winding corridors and Matthew chatted the whole while about their kind and just Master. He showed her his scarred wrist. "He will even heal you, if need be. Simply obey and all will be well. "

They stopped outside a large oak door, reinforced with iron strips. She could hear the sound of wind on the other side. The sound died the moment the key touched the lock. Torq opened the door and motioned Kaytlin inside, batting aside a vase that came flying at his head as if it were a gnat. Kaytlin ducked under his arm into the room and he slammed the door. An arctic blast of wind slammed Kaytlin against the wall and pinned her there, crushing the breath from her. Catarine eased around the end of the bed. She stopped in front of Kaytlin and glared at her.

"Who are you?" she growled softly. Kaytlin made a slight gasping noise and the wind eased off her. Just enough.

"Kaytlin." she choked. Catarine gasped and Kaytlin fell from the wall in a sudden absence of wind. She landed on her knees, coughing, at Catarine's feet.

"You are Kaytlin?" Catarine asked, reaching down to take her arm. Kaytlin nodded. "How can I be sure of that?"

"We've never met, so I have no proof to offer you." Kaytlin shrugged. "For that matter, how do I know you are really Catarine?"

Kathryn H. Sargeant   Blood Secrets: The Possession

"Well, when you put it that way, we certainly are in a bind." Catarine agreed, helping her to her feet.

"Except..."

"Go on."

"You were just controlling the wind. And Matthew told Jason we needed to get up higher to add the element of wind to our circle." Kaytlin said slowly. "How would he know that unless he knew you were wind? And would an imposter know that I knew you were." Catarine laughed, suddenly, and Kaytlin jumped.

"Enough, cousin. You think like my brother used to: in circles! I've no doubts, now." Catarine sat her down on the fainting couch and the wind picked up again, forming a bubble around them. "I don't want them to overhear us, I have a lot to tell you. Firstly, I attacked Krayboor's mind and found out quite a lot that you won't believe. Let me explain."

"My father was a half demon?" Kaytlin asked, incredulously. She sipped the warm wine that Catarine had poured for her and set the cup aside. Catarine nodded. "That makes me…"

"The daughter of two people who loved each other very much." Catarine said firmly.

"That explains why the black giant called me 'little sister'."

"That is why my father was so opposed to the union. He didn't know about you until you were well on your way. At first, he was going to kill you out of fear. Then, he lost Natahlia and his heart broke. He only wanted to care for you to make up for the wrong he had done to her, but he knew that if he pushed you like he had tried to push Natahlia, he'd lose you, too."

"Mother said that it was time for the circle to form, again. What did she mean?"

"Another demon tried to take over once before, a couple of centuries ago. Albaret, Shondea, Maxis, and Revad were the instruments of the elements that time. They destroyed him after a long battle, but had to sacrifice themselves to do it." Catarine looked at Kaytlin intently. "Is it any surprise that a priestess of Shondea would be one of the Circle, now?"

"A priestess of Shondea," Kaytlin mused. She raised her cup once more and smiled into the wine. "And a quarter demon."

"Did Krayboor make you drink a nepenthe?" Catarine asked suddenly. Kaytlin nodded. "You must be careful, then. It will erode your natural barriers to the demon blood. Cellestrar is used to increase dark powers."

"Really? Then, maybe we can use that to our advantage."

Kaytlin strode down the hall, swinging her hips as she walked. The new slit in her gown rose to her hip, revealing a tease of thigh and calf with every step she took. Her hair hung loose and lustrous down her back and her breasts strained at the tightened bodice of her gown. She turned a corner and stopped, pointing her bare toe and turning slightly sideways. In the corridor before her, Matthew and Maden were sitting on their haunches, throwing dice. She cleared her throat. Matthew's eyes traveled slowly up her tan leg, across her stomach and lingeringly over her breasts before finally reaching her face. He rose.

"Kaytlin, what are you doing here?" he asked. "I left you with Catarine."

"She bored me. And you didn't come back, so I melted the lock." she shrugged, the movement carefully emphasizing the rise of her breasts. "She's still there. I just couldn't take anymore of her blather." She sauntered over to them and pressed herself against Matthew's chest. "Want to play with me?"

"I knew that flower drink would screw up her mind." Maden said softly. "She's not even the same girl."

"Shut up, Maden." Matthew snapped, his arm curling around her waist. "Yes, pretty kitten, I'll play with you."

"Best you remember whose toy you are holding."

Matthew jumped as Torq materialized behind him. The giant's great hand closed on Matthew's shoulder and pulled them apart. Kaytlin pouted at him, the pupils of her eyes dancing flames of black. Torq grinned.

"The Cellestrar have released the demoness within." he nodded approvingly. "Go, little sister, before you get yourself into trouble." Kaytlin laughed, tossing her head saucily, and then sashayed away down the hall. She cast one last longing look at Matthew over her shoulder before she disappeared.

"How could a flower turn someone so completely around?" Maden asked, staring after her.

"Cellestrar amplifies the evil within. It erodes the good along with the memories." Torq glowered at Matthew. "You had best remember your place, lest you lose it, along with other parts."

"Should we let her roam free?" Maden asked. "I mean, she might hurt herself."

"I see no harm. More likely she'll hurt someone else. Let her be." Torq slowly faded until only his pointed grin was left hanging in the hall.

"I hate it when he does that." Maden shuddered.

"By noon, tomorrow we will reach the base of the range. On its other side lies the Valley of Osgaroth. That is where your castle sits." Mishala sketched in the soft earth at her feet and pointed to one scratch. "This is where the portal is: a passage through the mountains. We discovered them coming through it, so my mother ordered it sealed. The battle was fierce and many died, but we were able to seal it up."

"So, that is the way you mean for us to take?" Stephen demanded, peering hard over her shoulder. She nodded.

"We will unseal it. They won't expect that. But."

"But?"

"Mother died to close it. It may be very hard to open it, again." Mishala frowned.

"Mishala! An army marches this way!" a young girl came sprinting into the clearing. She doubled over, coughing. Mishala rose, shouting orders. Within seconds, there was no sign that anyone had been in that spot. From the safety of the trees, they waited with baited breath. Now, they could hear the sounds of horses' hooves moving closer. Mishala frowned and leaned her head close to Stephen, her lips next to his ear.

"This is strange. They have never used horses, before."

The riders broke through the trees below them and Stephen let out a whoop of joy. The royal colors of Regust blazed on banners and armor as the men reigned in. Stephen dropped to the ground before their leader, a grizzled veteran with black hair and full beard streaked heavily with grey. The soldier's horse danced sideways in surprise.

"Jalel! I have never been so happy to see you in my life!" Stephen shouted. Jalel slid from the saddle and threw his arms around the young man's shoulders. He crushed Stephen to his chest.

"When my King calls, I come!" he growled. "And I bring all the men I can."

"And how many is that?"

"Five hundred with me, I sent another five hundred to Lorell just in case it goes badly here, and another five hundred about a days ride behind." Jalel stepped back and an uneasy smile spread across his face. "Forgive me, my King. I was so overjoyed, I forgot myself."

"I expect nothing less from an old and dear friend, Jalel." Stephen laughed. He motioned to the trees. "These are men from my home. They are friends."

"Linara?" Jalel gasped as Mishala dropped at Stephen's side. She shook her head.

"She was slain. I am her daughter, Mishala, the new queen. Did you know Linara?" she asked gently. He nodded.

"From a long time ago. My condolences. You look much like her from her youth." he sighed, almost wistfully. Mishala twitched back her braid of ginger hai, and her pale blue eyes warmed with pleasure. Unconsciously, she brushed at the freckles across her nose. Jalel shook himself. "So, what is the plan, Stephen?"

Kathryn H. Sargeant   Blood Secrets: The Possession

"We will leave a squad here to lead the others to us at the base of the mountain. The rest of us will go on ahead and see if the pass can be unsealed. If it can't then we will devise another plan." Stephen declared. Mishala nodded.

"Nicora and several others will stay to serve as guides. Shall we go or do your men require rest?"

"We can ride further, my lady." Jalel assured her and then began barking commands at his men. Stephen turned to Kraig and Jason.

"Remind me, when we get home, to give Lorell a kingdom of her own. We are going to succeed. Mishala, will your warriors share our mounts? We may save some time by riding." he called and she nodded.

"We could be there by moon rise if we leave soon." she assured him. "We'll leave five amazons to each fifty men, in case we get separated in the dark. I will make the arrangements with my warriors." She strode off.

Kaytlin stood in the door, silhouetted by the torchlight behind her, her arms raised to grasp the doorframe on either side. Mikel watched her, expectantly, from the throne. Slowly, her arms dropped and she walked slowly into the room, her hips swinging enticingly from side to side. Mikel raised an eyebrow, questioningly as she faltered halfway to him, unsure of herself. It lasted only a moment and then her smile was brazen and brilliant as she continued on to skirt the pool of murky water at his feet and stand before him. He looked into her eyes and chuckled softly: Her pupils were black flickering flames in the deep pool of her blue eyes: the mark of a demoness.

"So, you have given yourself over to your father's blood?" he inquired, silkily. She ran a finger lazily around her throat and down her collarbone.

"Why deny what I am?" she asked huskily. "Your nepenthe was short lived, but it dissolved all those 'good and evil' rules they brainwashed me with. Destroyed all those barriers. It allowed me to learn so much more about myself than anyone would let me before." Kaytlin stretched out her hand to touch his lips. "About my wants." She stepped around to the side of the throne, sliding her fingers down to his throat. She leaned in to him, her lips next to his ear. "About my desires." Her fingers trailed down his arm. "My needs."

Mikel caught her wrist and twisted her around, pulling her onto his lap. She pouted, a cat robbed of its mouse. He gazed hard into her eyes and her fingers rose to twine in his hair, just behind his ear.

"And what needs are those?" he demanded, hoarsely. She lowered her eyes and smiled, bashfully, leaning her head into his shoulder.

"Power. Excitement. Riches. Pleasure." She punctuated each word with a biting kiss on his neck. "Why should I lock myself away in a cave when there is so much more to be gained in life?"

"True," he murmured, eyes half closed.

"And who better to teach me than you? We could learn so much from each other." she whispered, throatily.

"Indeed." Mikel tipped her head back and kissed her. She moaned against his mouth, parting her lips slightly. Mikel stood up and carried her from the room.

The full moon shone down with the force of a small sun, lighting the bare area around the base of the mountain. It rose in a sheer slice, unbroken except for the swell of one mammoth boulder at its base and stretched off in either direction as far as the eye could see. Kraig stared up at it and felt a twinge of despair in his stomach.

"Dreadful, isn't it?" Jason asked from behind him. Kraig nodded, unconsciously running his fingers along the rim of his shield.

"If we can't move that boulder, we will have to go around. That will take months. What will happen to them in that time?" Kraig shook his head, savagely. "It's my fault, Jason. I swore to protect her and I failed. I let him take her."

Kathryn H. Sargeant   Blood Secrets: The Possession

"And what of me? Why didn't I stop to wonder how Matthew knew we needed the element of air? No one ever spoke of Catarine's gift or mine. I could have easily been air for all he knew." Jason sighed. "She was right to choose you, Kraig, and you did not fail. We simply made mistakes. Tomorrow, I will move that boulder even if my head explodes like a ripe melon from the effort and we will fix our mistakes. Get some rest, now. We will need it for the coming battle." Kraig nodded and went to find a place to lie down. Jason approached the boulder. It was more like a small hill once you got close to it. Even if Kraig stood on his shoulders he would not be able to reach its top. Standing hand in hand, arms outstretched, it would take four people to reach the seals on either side. No wonder poor Linara died. Jason stared at the stone for a long time before he realized he was not alone. Stephen reached out and touched the cold rock with his fingertips.

"There is a river inside that mountain, Jason. I can hear it. When you move that boulder, the water will gush out and carve a path through the forest." he said.

"There's that much water there?"

"Yes, there's enough to start a whole new river."

"Is it just there or does it fill the whole mountain?" Jason asked, scratching his chin. Stephen moved a few feet away.

"The sound lessens here." Stephen counted three hundred paces and stopped. "I don't hear it at all here." Jason joined him, scratching his chin thoughtfully.

"You are positive?"

"Yes."

"Go get some rest. You'll need your strength tomorrow." Jason watched him go. When Stephen was out of sight, he sat down to face the mountain. Hesitantly, Jason laid both his palms flat against the cold rock and closed his eyes.

The door to Rose's room hung on broken hinges, the acrid smell of sulfur and smoke thick in the air. Mikel dropped Kaytlin from his arms to rush inside. She followed him at a more languid pace, stopping to lean against the doorjamb. She watched dispassionately as he tore through the destroyed room, searching for Rose. He righted the fainting couch and pulled what appeared to be a squashed sweet potato out from underneath it. He shook the creature by its wire hair until it roused and held it up to his face.

"What happened here? Where is the Lady Rose?" Mikel demanded. The creature blinked stupidly at him, then glanced over Mikel's shoulder. Terror distorted its hideous face as it began to squeak and writhe in his grasp.

"Her! Her! Her did this!" it shrieked in a tiny high-pitched voice. It gestured frantically at Kaytlin. She drew her lips back in a snarl and hissed at the creature. Mikel rounded on Kaytlin and she drew back.

"Why?" he demanded, shaking the creature at her. "Why did you do this?"

114

"Because." she hissed. He tossed the creature aside and closed the distance between them. Mikel grabbed her by the shoulders and shook her hard.

"Why?" he demanded again.

"Because, because she had everything I always wanted! And even now, a part of you wants her. She didn't deserve it. That's why. Besides," she grinned maliciously at him. "It was fun." Mikel stared at her for a long time, the silence broken only by the snuffling of the potato creature. Finally, Mikel spoke.

"Is she?"

"Dead?" Kaytlin nodded. "She ran around a lot, and she begged a lot, but she died just the same. It wasn't pretty." The potato tried to slip past her, and she kicked it viciously into the corridor. It hit the wall with a satisfying splat. Mikel stared at her.

"Go to your room, Kaytlin. You must learn that you cannot break your master's toys."

"But."

"Now!" he barked, shoving her back into the corridor. She glared at him, her fingers twitching at her sides. For a split second, he thought she would pounce on him like a cat. She lowered her eyes and turned away. "Kaytlin?" he called after her. She stopped and half turned. "You haven't done anything to Catarine?"

"Not yet." she snapped peevishly. He pointed a finger at her.

"Don't." he ordered. She shrugged, and walked away.

An excited murmur buzzed around his head like mayflies over a carcass. Jason groaned and forced his eyes open. Nicora bent over him, anxiously, her fingers probing his neck.

"I'm fine." he assured her, sitting up.

"What have you done?" she demanded in awe. He looked past her to the mountain. A tunnel high enough for riders to pass three abreast was burned through the mountainside. Warriors stood at its mouth, peering into the darkness.

"A direct route that no one will expect. We'll be there by tonight." he croaked. Kraig handed him a wineskin and he drank gratefully. Stephen clapped him on the back.

"Since everyone is here, we ride." he declared. Nicora frowned at Jason.

"You should not have strained yourself so much in so short a time. Who knows what effect this might have on your health."

"Thank you for your concern, friend, but I can rest as we ride. Now, let's get moving." Jason pulled himself to his feet and started toward the horses. Mishala laid a hand on Nicora's shoulder, following her sister's gaze.

"You are developing feelings for him, aren't you?" she asked softly. Nicora nodded. "Remember what Mother used to say: Men are slow of wit, quick of temper, and never appreciate the beauty before their eyes. His heart belongs to another, Nicci, and you are an Amazon."

"I know, Mishala." she sighed. "We will need torches. I will see what can be made." Mishala watched her head into the woods with a heavy heart. Nicora had pushed the men to keep riding so they could arrive earlier. Now, Mishala knew that it was not time that had spurred her on, but desire, and she was afraid of what painful roads that desire would take her sister down.

Soon, they were mounted and on their way. The passage was dry and straight, with a level floor. Jason had created the perfect passage for a march. He dozed on the back of Kraig's horse as it plodded along in the dim light. Stephen spoke softly to Mishala, discussing strategies for attack. In the darkness time stood still, and it seemed that they rode forever, yet never moved. And still, they rode on. Nicora walked beside Kraig's horse, her hand on its bridle.

"Tell me of this Kaytlin that you both care so much for," she requested. "It might make the time go by faster."

"Kaytlin? She's as sweet as summer honey, as hard willed as iron, as pure as a child's laugh, and as gentle as drifting snow." He touched the shield where it hung near the saddle horn. "She gave me this. It saved my life. And I'm the one who promised to save hers."

"And Stephen promised her mentor to save her. So many protectors." she sniffed sarcastically. "And how does Jason fit. Who did he promise?" Kraig looked down sharply, surprised at the bitterness in her tone.

"Himself. He's been watching over her since they were both children. His parents died when he was young, you see, and he took up residence in the woods near Caladren. He's been there ever since." Kraig shrugged. "You will like her, Nicora. You are a lot alike: Both of you are spirited and strong and gentle all at the same time. Neither of you would harm a fly if you didn't have to."

Kaytlin stretched elegantly on her stomach across the step below Mikel's throne, her fingers idly stroking the surface of the pool. The dress she had conjured to wear was nothing more than a sleeve of midnight silk, held together by thin golden cords at the sides. Her hair was pulled over one shoulder and her arms rested on it like a pillow. A sleek and graceful kitten, she turned dreamy eyes to the door.

"Come to play, Matthew?" she purred. He jumped, guiltily, and eased around the doorjamb where he'd been hiding. She watched him, vaguely amused, as he stood rooted in the doorway. "I'm waiting."

"Why here alone, kitten?" he demanded, huskily. She pushed herself up onto her forearms and cocked her head coquettishly.

"Master doesn't want to play, and I don't want to stay in my room. So, I look for new places to amuse myself." she licked her lips, invitingly. "I won't ask you, again, Matthew. If you want to play, play, if not go away."

Matthew looked around, nervously and she turned her face back to the ripples in the pool. Suddenly, he moved to her side, and she smiled expectantly up at him. Matthew pulled her up by her arm, and she melted against him with an inviting purr. He lowered his head to kiss her neck, and she arched her spine.

Her tiny moans spurred his desire, and his hands roamed over her ill-covered body, probing the gaps in the silken sides. Kaytlin ran her nails lightly across his back as he licked the hollow of her throat and she turned him slightly. She sunk her hands into his hair and pulled his head up so she could kiss his mouth, his chin, his ear. He groaned lustfully, his hands sliding up the backs of her thighs

"Do you know what we need, Matthew?" she breathed against his skin, nibbling at his neck.

"What's that, kitten?" he murmured.

"The element of air." Her teeth flashed as they sank into the soft flesh of his throat, severing and then tearing his windpipe out with a vicious twist of her head. He shoved her away and lost his balance on the edge of the step, his hands scrabbling desperately at his gaping throat. He splashed into the pool and tried to crawl away. She leapt on top of him, her foot on the back of his neck, pinning him in place. Matthew tried feebly to push her foot off as she stepped up onto his spine. Kaytlin watched impassively as his life's blood spilled into the pool. Matthew gave one final mighty shudder, and then was still. Kaytlin wiped the blood from her face and smiled.

Maden sat at the table, sipping from a tankard. The glow of the dying coals in the hearth pulsed like a heartbeat, first brightening and then dimming the cold room. He snorted into his cup. How had it come to this? He had always been a hire sword, like his older brother. He took the pay and did the job assigned to him, and he never looked back, never felt guilty. He took another gulp of ale. Why now? Why did Kaytlin haunt him? He wasn't responsible for her turn. It was her demon's blood that had turned her into the creature that had killed Rose, not him. But, he couldn't help remembering what she had been before he had gathered those flowers....

"Poor little Maden, sits all alone, no one to play with, in this cold room of stone," a voice sing-songed from behind him. He jumped, dropping his tankard. It rolled across the table and off the other side. Kaytlin laid her cool fingers against the back of his neck. "Poor little Maden, what runs through your mind? Is it a playmate you're hoping to find?"

"No, Kaytlin. I'm just trying to drown my regrets." he sighed. She went to pick up his tankard, and sat down across from him. As she slid it across the table to him it filled with a deep purple liquid. He lifted it to his face and sniffed. Kaytlin giggled.

"Do you think I would poison you?"

"You'd have every right." he said, then drained the entire tankard and slammed it onto the table. It refilled itself. The pulsing light reflected eerily against her eyes as she gazed at him. A ghost of a smile played about her lips.

"I wouldn't poison you, Maden. That's no fun." she assured him, leaning forward to trace the rim of the tankard with her finger. The simple wood shimmered and then gleamed. Maden stared at the silver chalice, its stem encrusted with bloodstones that now sat where his tankard had been. She grinned. "A fitting cup for the wine of a demon prince."

Kathryn H. Sargeant   Blood Secrets: The Possession

"I suppose saying I am sorry for all that's happened would be pointless." He lightly fingered a bloodstone and it began to glow softly at his touch. Maden raised his eyes and looked squarely into hers. "You were just supposed to be a job, Kaytlin. But I broke the first rule of being a mercenary. I liked you. I liked the way you seemed so worldly and still so naïve. The way you handled yourself. You were pure as spring rain. And I helped destroy that. I took the coins and promises of riches to come and I never thought beyond the moment."

"What is there to think about beyond right now?" she inquired softly.

"Tomorrow." he snorted. "There isn't going to be one, you know? Not for humanity. Demons will infest the world and humanity will become enslaved or wiped out. And it will be mostly my fault. And I will deserve to roast in the eternal fires. But, do you know the part that I truly cannot forgive myself for?"

Kaytlin shook her head.

"You." he said, simply, lowering his head. He stared at the scored tabletop, his shoulders shaking in mirthless laughter. "You. You never looked twice at me, pledged yourself to Kraig's protection. I don't think you ever said more than a handful of words to me in the time we were together. And helping to turn you into the she-demon that sits before me, now, is my greatest regret."

"Liar. You were never attracted to me. Your brother was."

"And I have never been able to take anything from Matthew. He wants you, still." Maden snatched up the goblet and drained it. It filled, again, as soon as it touched the table. Kaytlin's fingers curled around his wrist and her eyes widened until they filled the room, swirling black flames in a pulsing sea of blue.

"Maybe, little Maden, there could be a you and me. If you truly want to redeem yourself, well," she shrugged, "we shall see....."

Maden unlocked the door and shoved it open. Catarine looked up at him from the fainting couch and frowned.

"What do you want?" she demanded.

"Come. The guard is changing, we don't have much time. Go left down the corridor, down three flights of stairs. Go out the first door to your right. That's the courtyard. The stables are to the left. Wait for me there." he told her.

"How do I know this isn't a trap?" she asked, warily. Maden smiled.

"Christopher always called you his little sparrow." he winked. Catarine threw herself into his arms and hugged him tightly. After a moment, he shook her off.

"We're wasting precious time. Hurry. I'll be there, shortly." Maden locked the door behind them, and they each hurried off in a different direction. Catarine slid in and out of shadows and behind statues, keeping herself flat against the wall. She dashed down the curving stairs as quickly as she dared and eased the door to the courtyard open just a crack. The courtyard was deserted. She slipped out, easing the door closed, and dashed to the open stable door. She threw herself inside the dim interior and closed the door just as voices entered the courtyard. Guards. She moved into one of the empty stalls. Where was Maden? Had he been caught? Her heart pounded in her chest. Had someone discovered she was missing? No. There would be alarms if that happened. What about Kaytlin? She planned to give herself over to the demon blood. What if... No, she wouldn't think about Kaytlin, now. She would calm her heart and wait. One step at a time, that was all she could do. Catarine paced the stall, reaching absently to push back her hair. The sun would be peeking over the mountaintops soon. They were running out of time. Where was he? Suddenly, the door opened and Maden entered. He went straight to a horse and began saddling it. Catarine tiptoed over to him and laid a hand on his shoulder. With a savage oath, he spun to face her.

"Don't sneak up on me like that! Are you ready?"

"Yes. What took you so long?" she demanded as he pulled the cinch tight and turned to saddle another horse.

"I kept running into people that I couldn't ignore. Be ready in case we have to ride for it." He finished cinching her saddle and then gave her a boost up. She settled lightly and wrapped the reins tightly around her wrist. He led both horses from their stalls and mounted his, turning his horse to the door. "Remember, ride behind me and look docile. No matter what, do not react to anything." They left the stable and trotted across the courtyard to the main gate, where two demons atop the wall hailed them. Maden looked up at them in annoyance.

"Open the thrice cursed gate, already! The Master wants his lady to get some exercise. Apparently, being locked up doesn't suit her delicate nature." Maden sneered.

"Better hope she's not so delicate in the bridal chamber!" one of them called back, and they began to turn the stile that raised the gate. Maden laughed, his heart hammering inside his ribcage. Couldn't the damn creatures go any faster? What if Torq should pass by, or one of the damn potatoes decide to take Catarine her breakfast? After an eternity, the gate was up and he urged his mount through, tensed every moment for a shout of alarm. Catarine followed a few paces behind, her face a mask of complacency. They rode silently into the surrounding trees until they could no longer see the castle walls, and then nudged their mounts into a gallop. "Pray they are where she said they would be."

Kathryn H. Sargeant   Blood Secrets: The Possession

Kraig pushed himself off the ground and nodded at Nicora.

"Two horses, coming fast from the direction of the castle."

"We can deal with scouts." she said grimly before melting into the shadows. Jason crouched in the underbrush, his fingers pressed firmly into the dense earth. Kraig crouched beside him, shield at the ready. The sound of galloping hooves grew closer and closer, heading right for the spot where the two hid. Suddenly, the riders broke from the underbrush, horses screaming and plunging as the earth under their hooves suddenly rose like a wave and smashed into their sides. Cursing, the riders leapt from the falling mounts to roll and tangle in the brambles and vines. Stephen charged from the brush with a snarl and dove on top of the lead rider. Cursing, he pinned the flailing man to the ground and raised his dagger high overhead.

"Now, Maden, you son of a whore, you will pay for your treachery!"

"NO!" Catarine threw herself at him, knocking him sideways as Maden arced his body to throw Stephen aside. "That's not Maden! That's not Maden!"

Jason grabbed a struggling Maden by the hair and hauled him to his feet, but even as he stood, he was shifting. The form of Maden shimmered, then began to ooze, dripping like beeswax in the hot sun. Jason jerked his hand away to draw his dagger. Everyone stared in horrified fascination as the Maden creature began to shake, slinging off bits of skin like mud from a dogs pelt. Rose stepped from the oozing pile of her Maden disguise and helped Catarine to her feet.

"Isn't my little sister amazing? We don't have much time, we must prepare. The demon will come, and she will come with him."

Mikel glared at the empty room, flames dancing along his fingertips. One by one, the furniture began to explode, sending sparks and splinters careening throughout the enclosed space. A light, amused laugh rang out from the corridor and flooded the room. Cool fingers slid up his arm and soft lips pressed against his shoulder.

"Such a temper my demon lord has." Kaytlin giggled. He turned his head to glare down at her.

"Your games begin to annoy me, Kaytlin. What have you done with her?" he snarled. She raised an eyebrow, and stepped away, walking to the center of the room. She turned back to face him and grinned nastily.

"My games? My games? Your game made me what I am." she reminded him. "But, it is not my game that is being played here. Your humans turn against you; take your toys away."

"What are you saying?" he growled, advancing on her. She stood her ground, eyes flashing in challenge.

"Your faithful human, Maden. The very one who gathered your darling buds to turn me: he stole your precious lily maiden. They rode out together from the gates this very morning." she grinned. He stopped, stunned, and stared at her.

"Find me Matthew. He'll know where to look for his brother." he ordered. She shook her head.

"Oh, he won't be in much shape to help for a long while." Kaytlin tossed her head.

"What do you mean?"

"When you wouldn't play, I found someone who would." she shrugged. Mikel slapped her, spinning her around. She snapped back to face him, a high-pitched shriek coming from her mouth as she lunged at him with claws outspread. She slashed at his throat, but he caught her wrists and jerked them down. Her momentum sent her forehead crashing into his chin, and she blinked as the room spun.

"Taste discipline, little one, and remember your place." he hissed. Kaytlin screamed. The skin on her arms began to bubble and crack, blistering and baking along the bone. Blood evaporated in her veins, swelling them until they burst, sizzling muscle and steaming sinew. The heat raced up her neck and the smooth sweet flesh of her face began to ooze like melted tallow, her eyes to swell and her hair to smolder. She felt her heart slow as the muscles in her chest began to cook. Her tongue swelled, then split in two and her throat cracked open, steam escaping from her black charred lungs rolling out of her gaping windpipe.

Kaytlin fell to the floor, clutching her smooth white throat, and gasping air into her precious pink lungs. Tears poured down her smooth cheeks as she lay at his feet, and he stared down coldly at her. Whimpering, Kaytlin drug herself to his feet and began kissing the toes of his boots, pulling herself up by the leg of his breeches and then his tunic until she faced him, again.

"Forgive me, Master. Forgive me." she begged. "I will not forget my place, again."

"Oh, I am certain of that, Kaytlin." Mikel snapped. She stared up at him, reverently.

"The pool, great one." she whispered. "Can we not use the pool to locate them?" Mikel spun on his heel and marched out of the room, Kaytlin close at his heels like a puppy. "We can hunt them, like deer. Think of the sport. You like to hunt, don't you?"

"Quiet, girl." he snapped hurrying his pace. He stormed into the throne room and stalked to the pool. It lay black and motionless before the throne. Mikel passed his hand over it and the liquid began to ripple. The surface shimmered, and then settled on the smooth bare back of Catarine. She stood naked before a reclining Maden in the forest, the sound of a river burbling in the background. On the grass beside him amongst a pile of clothes lay a steaming goblet.

"He gave her the rest of the nepenthe." Kaytlin breathed. "No wonder she went with him so willingly."

"The fool. He didn't have brains enough to go far." Mikel snarled. "Torq! My horse!"

"Master, let me destroy him for you." she begged, clutching his arm as he started to turn away. "Please, let me prove my loyalty."

Kathryn H. Sargeant   Blood Secrets: The Possession

"Fine, but do not delay me," he growled.

"Oh, I won't, Master. I won't." she assured him, running from the room. He turned back to the pool, where Catarine was now curled against Maden, her fingers twining in his hair. Mikel stomped his foot into the water and the picture shattered.

Torq paced the hallways. Boredom. It was one thing he just could not stand. He would have to find something to do. Maybe he could find a nice dog to dismember, a human girl to torment. Something. Master was going off to destroy Maden, when he really should be seeing what kind of progress Stephen was making. Torq had no doubt that he, himself, could destroy the whelp, but Master wanted to suck his powers dry, first. Master was too caught up in his new flesh, in Torq's opinion.

Maybe a trip to the dungeon would cheer him. The echoes of torments past always lifted his morose spirits. He strolled the dark hallways with ease, taking the stairs down to the dungeons two at a time. His neck began to tingle as he reached the bottom landing. The smell of fresh blood hung thick in the air. Torq sprinted down the passageway, it's locked and rusted doors creaking in the wind his passage created. Shackles clanked against cold stone as he moved to very last door on the level. It stood partially ajar.

Torq shoved the iron door open and stepped inside.

Matthew hung from the shackles on the far wall, his head lolling backward, his throat grinning. Blood and water caked his clothing, turning them putrid and stiff. Hanging beside him by his ankles was Maden. His bare chest exposed a ragged gash from groin to throat and the knife that caused it lay inches below his trailing fingers. The pool of blood below him screamed of self-infliction.

Torq slowly began to smile. Then, he began to laugh.

Kaytlin urged her demon steed on, following closely on Mikel's heels. He had brought only a handful of guards with him to bring back the pieces. First, he would let Kaytlin slay the bastard. Then, he would have some real fun tormenting him over the ages. The things he could do with just a simple hair. Kaytlin adjusted the red and black cloak she was wearing so that it flowed over her shoulders, billowing out behind her. Her red leather tunic and breeches where criss-crossed with black leather. With her hair down and billowing, she looked like the living embodiment of flames. Mikel held up his hand, and they slowed their pace to a walk. He wanted to surprise the traitorous dog, so he wanted no hoof beats to alert them. The horses snorted in irritation. Mikel glanced at Kaytlin over his shoulder.

"Why do you tremble?" he asked, suspiciously.

"From anticipation, Master." she said, simply. "Should we go the rest of the way on foot? The steeds are restless." Mikel nodded, sliding neatly from the saddle. She held her arms out to him and he lifted her down. Kaytlin slid slowly down his body and he laughed softly.

"You just can't help yourself, can you?" he asked, lightly, and she shook her head. "Let's go." He turned and led the way into the trees, motioning his guards to fan out to either side. The sounds of the river were becoming louder as they walked and Kaytlin stumbled over a root. She dropped to her knees, her hand closing over the small emerald crescent moon that lay on the dirt. Mikel glanced over his shoulder at her.

Kathryn H. Sargeant   Blood Secrets: The Possession

With a loud rumble, the ground beneath his feet shifted, melted, and became hands that clutched at his knees, holding him in place. A rush of water encircled him and the wind rose in a mighty gale to crush the words from his lips. Kaytlin struggled to her feet and sent a bolt of flame toward him. Mikel grinned, but the grin died on his lips. The wind parted for the bolt and it smashed into his spine between his shoulder blades, immobilizing him.

Warriors crashed through the trees, attacking the demons that raced to their master's rescue. Kaytlin, Jason, Stephen, and Catarine advanced slowly on Mikel. Rose hurtled out of the trees, sword raised, and leapt over the circle of water to strike at him. With a triumphant laugh, he seized her by the hair and pulled her close, a shield against the others.

"Rose!" Kaytlin called, throwing the emerald moon. The wind caught it, and carried it straight into Rose's outstretched hand and she smashed it into Mikel's forehead. With an anguished roar, Mikel thrust her away and clawed at the gem burning into his skin. He dropped to his knees, head thrown back in agony, and the boy began to sputter, like a candle in a sudden breeze. Kaytlin watched in satisfaction as another shape imposed itself over Mikel, seemed to tear itself from his very body. Rose dashed away from him as the two separated and Mikel slumped to the ground, a broken heap. Over him, Krayboor raised his claws to the sky and roared. He gnashed razor teeth as he stretched. He turned to Kaytlin and pointed a talon at her.

"Have you forgotten your place already?" he growled, ominously. Kaytlin shook her head.

Kathryn H. Sargeant   Blood Secrets: The Possession

"I have always known my place." she snapped. "Now, you will learn yours." Black flames shot from her fingertips, engulfing the demon. He writhed in pain, and below him, Mikel whimpered and stirred. One of the amazons rolled into the circle of water and seized Mikel by the arms, pulling him across the boundary. And broke the protective circle. From the trees, arrows zinged into the melee. Kaytlin looked down in astonishment at the barb protruding from her shoulder, just above her left breast. She sank to her knees, breaking the line of flames, and they quickly died out. Krayboor leapt through the break in the circle and began wreaking havoc among the warriors, slashing and hacking with talons and tail and teeth. Kaytlin's head hit the ground and bounced in slow motion, and the death screams and clashing blades seemed so very far away to her, now. She stared straight ahead, too stunned to move, as a black foot came down on the dirt just in front of her face.

Jason slashed at the demons that rushed him, trying to reach the spot where Kaytlin had fallen. Stephen was racing after Krayboor, and Catarine was fighting off attackers of her own. Nicora leapt to his side, pressing her back against his.

"Some fun, huh?" she called, swinging her blade in a parry.

"I've got to get to Kaytlin. If she dies, we all die!" he yelled above the din.

"I'll go, you get to Catarine. She needs your help more than Kaytlin." Nicora pushed away from him and, using a falling demon for leverage, vaulted over the oncoming rush. She landed in a ducking roll, barely avoiding decapitation from a battle crazed Regustian, and came to her feet running. The large black demon stood with its back to Nicora, looking down at Kaytlin where she lay helpless at its feet. Even as she tried to run faster, it was leaning down toward the stunned girl.

Krayboor glanced at Kaytlin's crumpled form and laughed. Torq was going to shred the little bitch. He had come with reinforcements and they were fighting with merciless abandon. Krayboor would have to reward him well for this. He snatched up a warrior in his talons and ripped him apart, tossing the pieces idly at onrushing foes. Jason had reached Catarine and was dispatching her attackers. Somewhere off to the right, Stephen yelled hoarsely. He would enjoy this little stretch before he reclaimed the Regustian Prince's flesh. Then, he would resurrect his little lovelies and they would pleasure him throughout eternity.

A plume of water shot up before him, drenching him in a crashing wave. From behind, Stephen shouted, and the wind picked up around him, again.

Torq pulled the arrow from Kaytlin's shoulder and tossed it carelessly aside. She gasped as the shaft ripped out with a sharp pain that deepened into a warm, spreading sensation. Torq raised her to her feet, covering the wound with his hand.

"This is no time for napping, little sister. Your plan will never work if you only half try." he scolded, and a flash of light illuminated his hand. When he moved it away, the wound was gone, and so was any trace of blood.

"Why are you helping me?" she whispered.

"Because you amuse me, Kaytlin. Your wit, your games. You are full of surprises." he chuckled. "Now, here is a surprise of my own for you. You don't need to touch the others. Just concentrate on the same goal. Explore your demon side, and you'll see there's more than one plane of existence." Nicora hurtled toward his back, sword upraised. Torq winked out and her blade sliced through a grin hanging in midair. Kaytlin and Nicora stared at each other for a long moment, and Kaytlin nodded, reading her mind.

"You could strike me down, claim it was the demon. But, then the whole world would die. Is your love so great that you would sacrifice the world?" she asked. Nicora paled, shaking her head. Kaytlin smiled.

"Come, warrior, I need your help to kick some demon ass." Kaytlin closed her eyes, gathering all that she was and all that she could be from deep inside her. The demon blood in her pounded, shrieking to be released, and Kaytlin gave herself over to it with a final, deadly grace.

The wind tore at Krayboor, and earthen ropes twined around him, pulling him down. He ripped at the bindings, snarling and cursing. Stephen flung a net of waves over the monster, bearing him finally to the ground. Nicora raced to where Stephen, Catarine, and Jason stood, concentrating on keeping the beast immobile.

"Kaytlin is okay. She says when the signal comes, concentrate everything you have on this sword." Nicora drew the green and gold sword from the scabbard still belted at Stephen's waist and rested it lengthwise across the palms of her hands. "No matter what, you must not lose your concentration."

"What's the signal?" Jason demanded.

The world exploded in a brilliant flash of light.

There was a flash of blinding light. The landscape around her was devastation, littered with broken bodies and soaked with blood. The acrid smell of death and decay brought bile to her throat. Kaytlin stumbled, dragging the tip of the silver sword behind her in the dust. Was there no one left alive? Ahead of her, the ground heaved, and someone struggled to stand from the debris. Stephen. Covered in soot and soaked with blood. But alive! He stumbled backwards and she leapt to catch him. Her arms circled him and she dropped the sword as he struggled to free himself.

"Stephen, it's me! It's Kaytlin!" she cried. He twisted in her grip, eyes wild until they focused on her. He threw his arms around her in relief.

"Thank the gods! What happened? Did we end it?" he demanded. Kaytlin nodded. The sword began to shake in the dust. A small trickle of water ran down the blade, and tiny lines of earth marched across the hilt. The air around the sword pulsed, silently forming into a human hand that clutched the pommel, tightly. It lifted the sword from the ground to hover just between Stephen's shoulders. Kaytlin shuddered and a black flame ripped along the blade. Stephen's grip on her tightened and his eyes began to glow crimson, his lips wrinkling back from jagged teeth. His fingers began to elongate into claws.

"Thank the gods." Kaytlin whispered, as the flames wrapped around the hand and it plunged the sword through them both.

Bodies littered the ground. Kraig groaned, rubbing his eyes and sat up. His first sight was Kaytlin in her blood colored clothes standing erect in the midst of the broken field. She stumbled, dragging her arm behind as though she were carrying something heavy. He watched in horror as first she stumbled, and then raced to Krayboor's side. The monster turned toward her, arms outstretched. Kraig glanced at the others; they were just standing in a semi-circle, staring at the sword Kaytlin's mother had given her. Why didn't they do something? Why didn't they stop her? Suddenly, the sword lifted into the air, held aloft by a hand made of wind and sliced through the air, toward the monster. Kaytlin stepped into the creature's embrace and held it tightly. The blade of the sword erupted into black flames, and then buried itself into the monsters back and right through Kaytlin's ribcage. The monster roared, shoving her away, and she dropped to her knees, the sword sliding free of her body with a sickening wet sound. She toppled backwards to the ground.

Krayboor staggered back from her, his tail thrashing as he tried to reach the hilt of the sword. Flames poured from his mouth and ears, his yellow eyes bulging from the pressure inside his head. The skin of his face rippled as veins of water tore through his tissues like gouging fingers. Deep, rich earth trickled from his nose. His claws began to crack and split, forced open by wind trying to escape the confines of his body. He shrieked, spinning around, looking for salvation. A grin floated in the air behind him. Krayboor howled. Suddenly, his eyes exploded in a flash of gore and flames licked his empty eye sockets from within. He dropped to his knees, and with a final enraged roar, he crumpled to

138

the ground where the flames consumed him from inside. In seconds, only a pile of muddy ashes was left.

They ran to Kaytlin's side. She lay on the ground, hands pressed to the gaping wound in her chest. Kraig dropped to his knees beside her, and cradled her head in his lap, and Catarine threw herself to the ground to press her cheek to Kaytlin's. Her tears dropped onto Kaytlin's colorless face. Jason and Stephen stood staring down at her limp form in sorrow.

"She sacrificed her humanity for our escape, and her life for our survival." Rose said softly from beside Stephen. "We will build her a shrine like no other before."

"Mikel!" Stephen gasped, suddenly remembering his brother. Rose put a reassuring hand on his arm.

"He is going to be alright. Nicora is with him, now."

Kaytlin's body jerked and she gasped, a long drawn out gulp of air. Convulsions rocked her body and Catarine threw herself on top of her to hold her down. After several moments she lay still, again. Only now there was a faint hint of color to her face. They looked at each other uncertainly, and then Kraig choked back a sob. Kaytlin's eyelids fluttered and a groan escaped her lips. Catarine pushed her hands away from the wound and cried out with joy. A long pale scar showed lightly against Kaytlin's skin, and then disappeared altogether.

"What's everyone staring at?" Kaytlin asked, shifting uncomfortably.

Kaytlin leaned against the wall of the house, her face pressed against the cool stone. They had been riding for long weeks, finally reaching Ariangard just before the first snows, and she was tired. The great battle songs never said anything about the tiring ride home. Someone stirred in the shadows behind her. He had had a rougher ride than she. She turned back to the cot and laid a comforting hand on his brow. Mikel blinked up at her in the dim interior light and tried to smile.

"It only hurts when I breathe." he said, trying for a light tone. She sat on the edge of the bed and took his clammy hand in her own.

"It will take a long while to regain your health. You must be patient," she told him, earnestly.

"Well, I'm not going to be running off to join any battles any time soon," he assured her. "How are you?"

"Tired. Sore. Raging inside." she shrugged.

"We both know what it's like to fight the demon within." he muttered. "I did try to fight."

"I know." she assured him, tenderly touching his face.

"Get back in bed!" Catarine ordered from the door. She carried a large tray with a pitcher of fresh milk and bread and cheese on it to the small table between the two beds. She set it down carefully and then rounded on Kaytlin. "You shouldn't be up, you should be resting. Now, get back in bed before I have the boys tie you to the posts!"

Kathryn H. Sargeant   Blood Secrets: The Possession

"Stephen's going to have his hands full with her." Mikel remarked wryly. Kaytlin climbed silently back into bed and let Catarine fuss over her. As soon as they were both fed and resting, Catarine left them. There was a soft knock at the door and Jason entered to stand at the side of Kaytlin's bed.

"You look everywhere but my eyes, Jason. Why?" she demanded, tiredly.

"They unnerve me, now." he admitted, sheepishly. "So does the memory of seeing you die and come back."

"I am not the same girl I was and I cannot pretend to be. Do you still claim to love me?" she asked. He hesitated a brief moment and then nodded slowly, swallowing hard. She read the hopelessness in his eyes and she smiled, reassuringly. "Just not the same way: and that is all for the best, my friend. Love me as a sister and no more. Nicora is more deserving of your attentions, anyway. She loves you with all her heart."

"She does?" he asked sharply, glancing up in surprise. His eyes met hers, and he shuddered, involuntarily. She nodded.

"Yes. Why else would she choose to 'escort' us back to Ariangard? Go find her, Jason, she won't be far away. Go be happy. I am." she insisted. He leaned down and kissed her cheek, pausing to murmur in her ear. She nodded, and he turned away, leaving quickly. She met Mikel's questioning eyes across the table and shrugged.

"He asked if we were still friends. I said yes."

Kathryn H. Sargeant   Blood Secrets: The Possession

"I told Rose the same when I left her in Silver Wood. Let Stephen and Catarine rule long and justly over both kingdoms. Rose wanted to train with the amazons. I will choose my own path as well." he nodded.

"Perhaps when you are well you can become an instructor at Lorell's academy." she suggested.

"Perhaps. She is an amazing fighter. Stephen was disappointed that she chose leading a school over leading his men. Boys and girls from all areas will come for her tutelage. Tell me, Kaytlin, what will you do?" he asked, settling back against the pillow. She stared at the ceiling.

"I don't know. My home is gone. I guess I will have to search for another." she murmured. "Let me say what we both keep dancing around: We can't stay here. They don't want us because we were both touched by the demon. They don't trust us."

The door opened, and Kraig slipped in and eased it closed.

"We're not asleep, Kraig, no need to be so secretive." Mikel chuckled.

"It's not you I'm afraid of rousing. Catarine is manic about no one disturbing you. She'll skin me alive if she catches me in here." he whispered.

"So, what would make you risk such a fate?" Kaytlin demanded. Kraig walked to her bedside, his arm behind his back, and stood there. With a sudden flourish, he whipped a handful of wildflowers from behind his back and held them out to her. She laughed and took them from him, plopping them in the half empty milk pitcher. "My thanks." Kraig gazed long into her eyes, searching.

"How do you truly feel? Is there anything I can do or get you?" he asked. She shook her head.

"My eyes don't bother you?" she asked, gently.

"I don't see any difference. They were spell-binding before, they are spell-binding now." he shrugged, and then turned to Mikel. "And how are you?"

"Well as can be expected." Mikel grinned and light glinted off his forehead.

"That emerald moon is going to be hard to conceal, maybe we can use a fine powder to dim it." Kraig offered. Mikel touched the stone in the center of his forehead and shook his head.

"I rather like it. There's not another person in the world that has an emerald fused to their forehead. Makes me unique." Mikel announced with a smile. The emerald flashed into Kaytlin's flame-pupils and she laughed, suddenly. They turned to her and she blushed.

"A vision just came to me: Three traveler's upon a road leading to sunset. One, a gleam of emerald; the next a gleam of flame and the third with a shield of silver and green. Our adventures are not yet over, my friends." she said, reaching for Kraig's hand. He took it and then reached for Mikel's.

"There are no two others I would rather travel with." he told them solemnly, closing his fingers around Mikel's.

"Nor I." Mikel agreed.

"Nor I." Kaytlin's eyes glowed slightly, casting pale shadows around the room.

Kathryn H. Sargeant   Blood Secrets: The Possession

"It's settled, then. Come spring, we will both be restored to health. The three of us will set off then." Mikel announced. "Agreed?"

"Agreed." they chorused.

"Well, Kraig, you've a lot of work ahead of you. You have to get mounts, and clothes and supplies," Kaytlin sighed, closing her eyes. Her voice trailed off as she drifted off to sleep. Mikel raised an eyebrow, at Kraig.

"I hope she stays awake a little better on watch."

Outside the window, a sharp-toothed grin floated in mid-air.